The little girl was adorable

Allison gave her a second look. She seemed familiar. But Allison couldn't have met her before. The red wagon in the driveway had Connecticut plates.

She glanced back at the father. Definitely she hadn't seen *him* before. She would have remembered. He was slender and tall and moved with a natural grace that reminded her of John F. Kennedy, from the old footage she'd seen on TV.

She watched as he scooped up his daughter onto his shoulders, then paused to talk to the movers for a minute. Next, he went to the garage and pulled out the tricycle. Gently he set the girl onto the seat.

"Give it a try," he urged her. And then his gaze met Allison's.

Dear Reader,

Welcome to a new trilogy about three brothers who have been very unlucky in love. The eldest, defense attorney Matthew Gray, is a self-professed workaholic, whose marriage is unraveling before his eyes. Meanwhile, commitment-phobic Nick, the youngest of the Gray brothers, switches girlfriends about as often as his shifts with the Hartford Police Department.

Which leaves us with the middle brother, Gavin Gray. Gavin has always been the peacemaker in the family...which might explain why all the women in his life have been so needy.

All the women, that is, except his new next-door neighbor, Allison Bennett. I hope you enjoy reading this story and finding out what happens when Gavin meets successful interior designer Allison. Her specialty is fixing up houses, but in Gavin's case, the project turns into something much, much more.

I love hearing from readers, and this includes you! Please contact me through my Web site at www.cjcarmichael.com. Or mail me a letter through my publisher. Either way works!

Happy reading,

C.J. Carmichael

THE DAD NEXT DOOR
C.J. Carmichael

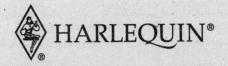

HARLEQUIN®

TORONTO • NEW YORK • LONDON
AMSTERDAM • PARIS • SYDNEY • HAMBURG
STOCKHOLM • ATHENS • TOKYO • MILAN • MADRID
PRAGUE • WARSAW • BUDAPEST • AUCKLAND

ISBN-13: 978-0-373-71471-1
ISBN-10: 0-373-71471-8

THE DAD NEXT DOOR

www.eHarlequin.com

Printed in U.S.A.

ABOUT THE AUTHOR

Hard to imagine a more glamorous life than being an accountant, isn't it? Still, C.J. Carmichael gave up the thrills of income tax forms and double entry bookkeeping when she sold her first book in 1998. She has now written over twenty novels for Harlequin Books and strongly suggests you look elsewhere for financial planning advice.

Books by C.J. Carmichael

HARLEQUIN SUPERROMANCE

HARLEQUIN SIGNATURE SAGA

HARLEQUIN NEXT

*Return to Summer Island

For Laura Shin

In appreciation of all the books we have worked on together and all that you have taught me.

CHAPTER ONE

THE EMPTY SEATS in his station wagon haunted Gavin Gray as he drove up to the biggest house on the crescent. He stopped the car and gazed through the windshield at the classic Cape Cod colonial. The house looked a little tired. Welcome to the club. But it had good bones. Cindy Buchanan, his real-estate agent, beckoned to him from the door.

"You have to see this one. It's a real family home."

Cindy was a friendly, plump woman in her midfifties. She'd been showing Gavin houses all day, her patience never wavering. He was sure she'd have felt terrible if she knew how much pain her cheerful words had just brought him.

A family home.

He turned around to face what was left of his family—one little girl strapped into a booster chair in the middle of the backseat. "Tory? Want to see another house?"

Predictably, his daughter offered no opinion, but she scrambled out willingly and held his hand as he led her up the sidewalk to the welcoming front porch.

"It has a huge pie-shaped yard. And it's the only house on this road that backs onto the lake." Seeing his concerned frown in reaction to her comment, Cindy added quickly, "But there's a fence, so it's perfectly safe."

He walked through the rooms, hardly noticing the details. But then he stopped cold at the sight of the view from the kitchen windows. It was fabulous.

On Golden Pond had been filmed at Squam Lake and the town had never forgotten its moment of cinematic glory. Gavin had seen signs on the main road guiding tourists to the actual sites used in the movie.

"The house does need a little work." Cindy ran a hand over a crack in the kitchen wall. "It's changed owners several times in the past few years. You should have seen it when Old Man McLaughlin was still alive."

He couldn't have heard that correctly. "Did you say McLaughlin?"

"That's right. It was just Adele and her daughter living here in the end. And when Marianne left home…"

He felt as if he'd been submerged in ice water. He couldn't breathe. Was his heart still beating? "Marianne McLaughlin used to live here?"

"Yes. Do you know her?"

How many times had he asked himself that question? The ultimate answer being that he couldn't have. But he wasn't about to share that insight with Cindy Buchanan.

He looked around with sharpened interest, trying to picture the beautiful, remote woman in this place. "I used to, but I haven't seen her in about six years."

His breathing returned to normal as he contemplated the significance of what he'd just learned. Could it possibly be this easy? "Do you know where Marianne's living now?"

"Afraid not. She came back once, to bury her mother in the family plot. I haven't heard anything about her since then. But maybe someone in town has. How did you say you know her?"

He hadn't. And he wouldn't. "We were friends."

"Quite the beautiful girl."

True enough. Where looks were concerned, Marianne could not be beat.

Tory came round the corner then, moving so quietly that Cindy didn't even notice her. His daughter had been wandering upstairs, checking out the bedrooms, but Gavin knew that if he asked her whether she liked what she'd seen, Tory wouldn't have anything to say. Even when Samantha was alive she'd been reluctant to express an opinion, relying on her twin to do it for her.

He decided to try anyway. "So, what do you think?"

Cindy turned in time to see Tory shrug. The real-estate agent's thin eyebrows rose in surprise. "Speaking of the devil, your daughter looks remarkably like…"

"I think I've seen enough." He wasn't interested in taking the conversation in that direction. Besides, he really had seen enough. The house was in need of work, but it was on a quiet street and the link to Marianne was a coincidence that couldn't be ignored.

"I'd like to make an offer."

Cindy Buchanan looked surprised but pleased.

ON ALLISON BENNETT'S thirtieth birthday she found a special delivery package on her front porch. It wasn't a birthday gift, though. The return address was from Abby's Print Shop in North Conway.

Darn. The wedding invitations.

She'd meant to cancel the order, but there'd been a lot of cancellations to take care of in the past two weeks and she'd dropped the ball on this one.

Breaking off an engagement six weeks before the wedding was a pain in the butt.

Since there was no sending them back at this point, she ripped open the box and pulled out one of the printed cards. They were lovely.... Buff card stock, silver print, very elegant. Avoiding a loose board she'd been meaning to fix, Allison sat on the front porch step to take a closer look.

Allison Moore Bennett and Tyler Paul Jenkins cordially request your presence...

She remembered the afternoon that she and Tyler had ordered these. They'd argued over the wording. Tyler had wanted traditional invitations, while she'd been in favor of something more casual. She read through the rest of it. The ceremony at the chapel on Church Island at three.

Canceled. Reception to follow at the Lakeside Inn. Also canceled.

She sighed, and then lifted her head at the sound of heavy footsteps out on the street. New owners were moving into the McLaughlins' old house today. Two men in baggy jeans and dark T-shirts carried a sofa from the moving van down the ramp and in through the front door. They'd been hard at work for over an hour and now the van was nearly empty.

Allison had been keeping tabs on their progress, though somehow she'd missed the arrival of the family itself. The new owners were already inside, she surmised from the red station wagon parked next to the garage, which was being used as an unloading area for all sorts of things. A lawn mower, a canoe, a mountain bike, a cherry-red tricycle...

She hadn't been snooping. It was just that she'd had a number of chores to take care of out here this afternoon. The late summer sunshine was perfect for watering plants, sweeping the porch and shaking the cushions on her outdoor furniture.

Okay, she *was* snooping. But she couldn't help being curious. The house next door, 11 Robin Crescent, had always been Allison's idea of the perfect family home. It was larger than hers, a lovely colonial complete with a copper weather vane on the roof. Best of all, it backed onto the lake. When she was growing up, living on the other side of town, she'd spent a lot of time in that house.

Her somber mood returned as she thought of her childhood friend Marianne. They'd had fun together. They both loved art, though her talent had been no match for Marianne's. And they'd spent hours in the sun and swimming together behind that house.

But somehow the good memories were always overtaken by the bad ones. Allison tried not to think of those as often. It was easier now that Marianne didn't live here anymore. She'd moved away years ago, leaving her mother alone in that house until the day she died. Since then, several other families had taken up residence. But none had stayed longer than a year or two.

Allison had watched them come and go with envy. If she had had the money, she would have loved to buy the house herself. But she'd been lucky to afford the one she had—thanks to an inheritance from her grandmother.

The movers emerged from the house next door

again. Instead of unloading more furniture and boxes, they grabbed brown bags from the cab of the van. A late-afternoon snack.

Allison realized she was hungry, too. Time to start dinner. Just as she was heading inside, though, her new neighbor and his young daughter made an appearance. He was a nice-looking man, about her age or maybe a few years older.

The girl was adorable. Allison gave her a second look—she seemed familiar. But Allison couldn't have met her before. The red wagon in the driveway had Connecticut plates.

She glanced back at the father. Definitely she hadn't seen *him* before. She would have remembered. He was slender and tall and moved with a natural grace that reminded her of John F. Kennedy, from the old footage she'd seen on TV.

Allison watched as the man scooped his daughter onto his shoulders, then paused to talk to the movers. Next, he went to the garage and pulled out the tricycle. Gently, he set the girl onto the seat.

"Give it a try," he urged. And then his gaze met Allison's.

She left the opened box of invitations on her porch and went to meet him halfway. "Hi!

Welcome to the neighborhood. I'm Allison Bennett."

He hadn't shaved for a few days. Lucky for him, he was one of those men who managed to look sexy, rather than unkempt, as a result.

He offered a tired smile and shook her hand. "Thanks. It's good to be here, finally. I'm Gavin Gray. And this is my daughter, Tory."

Allison squatted to say hello, but the young girl wouldn't look at her.

"Tory? Can you say hi to our new neighbor?"

Apparently not. She pedaled off down the sidewalk as if she hadn't heard her father's request.

That was when Allison placed the resemblance. Tory Gray looked a *lot* like Marianne McLaughlin had at that age. Dark hair, glowing skin and wide blue eyes. A miniature Snow White.

Even as a small child, Marianne's beauty had worked to her advantage. In kindergarten, the little boys were forever sharing their lunchbox treats with her and all the girls scrambled to be her partner during gym and class projects.

Allison wondered if Tory's grade-school years would be equally blessed.

"I'm sorry." Gavin apologized for his daughter's behavior. "She doesn't mean to be rude. She's just shy."

"That's okay. Is she starting grade one this year?"

He nodded, keeping his eye on the child. When she reached the end of the block, she turned the trike around and started back for home.

With the full sun in Gavin's face, Allison saw lines around his eyes and mouth that she hadn't noticed before. He didn't just seem tired. He looked sad.

For that matter, so did Tory. She pushed the pedals on her tricycle grimly. No trace of pleasure on her pretty face.

"So…" Gavin began. "How long have you lived here?"

"In Squam Lake, all my life. But only in this house a few years." Allison chatted about the town for a while, and Gavin explained that he was an architect, with plans to support himself here designing cottages.

"I used to work at a downtown office in Hartford, but I want to be around for Tory as much as possible. Provided I can line up enough clients to keep bread on the table."

Admirable goals for a father. Only where

was the mom? Inside unpacking? Gavin might think she was prying if she asked. Worse yet, if he was a single dad, he might think she was hitting on him.

"I should get going. I was about to make dinner." She took a few steps toward her house. "Do you and Tory like lasagna? I'm having it for dinner and I always make extra. I'd be happy to bring over a casserole."

Tory stopped her tricycle by her father's feet. He held her hand as she got off. "What about it, Tory? Would you like lasagna for dinner?"

She looked at her father mutely. Gavin seemed disappointed by her silence, but also resigned— as if he'd expected nothing more. He forced a smile that didn't reach his eyes. "If it isn't too much trouble, that would be great."

As soon as she stepped inside her house, Allison's phone began to ring. The call was from one of the older women who lived on the block, Gertie Atwater. Gertie was an old friend of her mother's, and she'd once worked for Allison's grandmother, too. She still put in three afternoon shifts a week at The Perfect Thing.

"Well? What's he like? I saw you talking to him."

"He seemed…pleasant." It wasn't exactly the right description, but Allison couldn't put words to the impression Gavin and his daughter had made on her.

"He's certainly good-looking. And his daughter is a doll." And then, most importantly, Gertie added, "There isn't any wife in the picture, you know."

Allison almost asked her how she knew that, but then she stopped. Of course Gertie would have quizzed Cindy Buchanan, the real-estate agent who'd sold the property.

Allison didn't think the people who lived in Squam Lake were nosier than people in any other small town in America. But this was the sort of place where neighbors watched out for one another. At times—like now—they could seem to care just a little too much.

After Gertie's call, Allison pulled out her mother's recipe for lasagna. No sooner were the onions and garlic sautéing for the tomato sauce, than the phone rang again.

This time it was her dad. "Hello, sweetheart. Happy birthday. Are you having a good day?"

Without leaving time for an answer, he added, "Have you heard from Tyler?"

"He called to wish me a happy birthday," she admitted. "But he was just being polite." She had to make that completely clear, since her dad was having difficulty accepting her broken engagement.

"He still loves you."

"I don't…"

"It's not too late to go through with the wedding. Tyler's a nice guy, with a successful business. He'd be a good provider."

"Dad, I can take care of myself."

"Sure you can," her father said. But she knew that despite the fact that she'd lived on her own for years and ran a successful business, he didn't really believe that. He'd always been protective, and he'd become even more so since he and her mother divorced.

"I'm okay on my own, Dad. Honestly."

He sighed and she could tell he was giving up on the lecture—for now. "We still on for dinner?"

"Of course. I'm bringing lasagna." Even after all these years alone, her father had not learned how to cook for himself.

"Good. I bought a nice cake from the bakery.

It's chocolate—your favorite. We'll have a real celebration."

"Thanks, Dad. I'm looking forward to it." She heard the beep that told her another call was waiting. This time it was her mother, in New York City.

"I've bought you a plane ticket to come and visit us for Thanksgiving. We'll do some shopping. Take in a few shows."

"That sounds wonderful." She got along well with her stepfather and he was always tactful enough to make sure she had plenty of one-on-one time with her mom.

"In the meantime, are you sure you're okay? I could take some time off from my job if you needed me."

It was a generous offer, Allison knew. Her mother hadn't returned to Squam Lake since the divorce. She hadn't said anything, but Allison guessed the memories were too painful.

"Mom, I'm fine."

"Okay. If you say you're fine, then I believe you. Have a wonderful day, sweetheart. You deserve it."

"I will. Love you, Mom. Talk to you next week."

As she returned to her cooking, Allison

thought about her parents. It had always bothered her that they'd given her no reason for ending their marriage. She supposed they were trying to shelter her. But she'd been an adult when they'd separated. Old enough to handle the truth.

Unlike the little girl next door. She'd made such a job out of riding that tricycle. Was a divorce the reason for the sadness in her eyes?

And her father's, too?

CHAPTER TWO

MONDAY MORNING, Gavin woke up with a sick feeling in his stomach. It was hard not to think about the little girl who wouldn't be starting grade one today. His little Samantha…

He took a moment to remember her, gazing at the photo of the twins that he kept by his bed.

Then he pulled himself to his feet, went to the washroom and forced himself to smile at his image in the mirror.

Just the act of smiling, according to research, made you feel happier. He wasn't so sure about that, but he kept trying, nonetheless.

When he'd finished washing and dressing, he went to Tory's room to help her select an outfit for her first day. She was already awake, sitting on her bed and staring woefully at her dresser.

"Would you rather wear shorts or a dress?"

No answer.

"Pink or blue?"

Tory just stared at him.

So, as usual, he set out some clothes, then made her breakfast. They walked to school together, met the principal and were shown to the first-grade classroom. He wasn't surprised when Tory cried as he tried to leave her with her new teacher, and he ended up staying in the classroom for the first hour and a half. At recess, the teacher encouraged him to leave.

"I'll call if Tory doesn't settle in after you're gone."

Gavin returned to the house on Robin Crescent. Stepping around open boxes, he made his way to the kitchen. The movers had placed the table and chairs in the alcove overlooking the lake and now he sat and pivoted so he could look out over the water.

There was much to do, yet he felt paralyzed.

Over the weekend he'd assembled Tory's bed, unpacked her clothing and set up her dollhouse. Even so, her room looked bleak. It could do with a coat of paint, at the very least.

The rest of the house needed work, too. At some point he'd have to fix the cracks in the walls and replace the grimy light fixtures and worn carpets. Maybe he should have bought a place in better repair.

He still couldn't believe that he and Tory were living in the house in which Marianne had grown up. Many times she must have sat in this exact spot. He tried to imagine what a teenaged Marianne would have thought about as she looked out onto the lake. But he couldn't. He'd never been able to understand what went on in her head.

He certainly couldn't understand the way she'd left their kids, never looking back, never phoning or writing or making any contact at all. They'd been one-year-olds. To him so sweet and adorable. He couldn't imagine leaving them. At least not by choice.

Which had led him to wonder if Marianne was dead. But his calls to hospitals and police stations in the area had turned up nothing.

For a while he'd considered hiring an investigator, but his brothers had talked him out of it.

"She knows where you are," Nick, ever the hard-nosed cop, had pointed out. "If she doesn't care enough to keep in touch, you and the girls are better off without her."

Gavin had tried to accept his brother's advice.

But Samantha's death had set him thinking about Marianne again. He wondered what she'd been doing with her life for the past six years. How was she earning a living? Had she found a man who made her happy?

And what would she say when she found out about Sam's death? Would she finally be sorry? Would she regret leaving all those years ago?

Most importantly, would she realize how much Tory needed her now? Sam's death had hit the poor kid so hard. Gavin hated knowing how much his daughter hurt. The pain was hard enough for him to handle. How could a child be expected to cope?

He rubbed a hand over his face.

An hour went by. There was no call from the school. He hoped that meant that Tory was settling in.

Light danced on the lake. A pair of ducks landed on the water, then drifted out of view. The pain in his chest seemed to ease a little. He took a deep breath, grateful for the respite.

Another hour went by.

In the first months after Sam's accident, many days had passed this way, with Gavin simply sitting, staring into space, accomplishing nothing aside from the immediate chores required to care for Tory.

Reminding himself that he wasn't going to live that way anymore, Gavin finally dislodged himself from his chair. He sorted through boxes until he found the ones from his old office. Since he had a new house to pay for and a daughter to support, this seemed like a good place to start.

In the upstairs room he'd chosen for his workspace, he assembled the legs on his drafting table, then set up lamps and unpacked his office chair. Next, he ripped open one of the moving cartons and found his files.

By the time he had them organized in his filing cabinet, it was shortly after two. He set the alarm on his watch so he wouldn't forget to pick Tory up from school at three-thirty.

As he stacked books on the windowsill, a movement outside caught his attention. The cute neighbor who lived next door and made such good lasagna was coming home.

The lush green leaves of a big oak tree partially obscured his view. Still, he managed a glimpse of her light-blue dress as she unlatched her gate and crossed to her porch. By the time she reached the door, he couldn't see her.

She'd been friendly the other day, but not too friendly. He was glad about that. He wanted to get along with his new neighbors, but that was all. He wasn't ready for anything more. Certainly nothing romantic. Since Marianne had left, he hadn't had time to think about women. And since Sam… He hadn't had the heart.

Sure, Allison Bennett was pretty. And she seemed kind and thoughtful. Maybe at some other point in his life he'd have considered asking her out. But this just wasn't the time.

There was that casserole dish to return, however.

He'd put it in the dishwasher last night. Now he ran downstairs and pulled it out, relieved to find it was spotless. He might as well take it back before he forgot.

Gavin left his house, passing by the old oak en route to Allison's. The tree was one of several that bordered the road, branches arcing over the pavement to form a natural bridge from one side of the street to the green patch in the middle.

Robin Crescent was going to be breathtaking in a couple of weeks, when the leaves began to change. Living in New England, you couldn't help but love the fall. Still, Gavin's sense of anticipation for the coming season was marred by the memory of how much Marianne had hated it.

"Why does everyone think autumn is so beautiful? The leaves are dying. Don't you think it's sad?"

She'd had empathy enough for the trees. Why not for her own daughters?

Frustrated to find himself dwelling on the past again, Gavin rapped on his neighbor's door a little harder than he'd intended to.

Allison responded at once. She was shaking her hair out of a ponytail and he had an unanticipated visceral reaction as her shiny maple syrup–colored hair fell loose to frame her face.

He resisted the impulse to touch it. Instead, he held out the baking dish. "Thanks very much. The lasagna was great."

"You're welcome. I'm glad you liked it."

He found it hard dealing with new people—people who didn't know about the tragedy. His daughter's death wasn't the sort of background information you could casually insert into a conversation, like telling someone you were an architect.

"Nice place." He glanced around, admiring everything he could see from the foyer. Warm colors, interesting artwork, an intriguing French country armoire.

Allison's house wasn't showroom perfect, like the rooms the designers at his old firm used to create. This simply felt like a home. He needed to fix up his new place like this. Yet he felt overwhelmed by all the work it would take to pull it off. "Did you use a decorator?"

"Didn't need to. That's what I do—I work out of my shop downtown. You may have noticed it. The Perfect Thing?"

He was impressed. "That's yours? We walked by on Saturday when we were looking for a café. You've got lots of beautiful stuff."

"Thank you. The shop used to be my grandmother's. When I was a kid, I would hang out with her on weekends. I thought I was a big help—at least my grandma made me feel as if I was."

She smiled, obviously thinking of happy memories, and then she stuffed a folder of papers into a leather tote bag. He recognized them as architectural drawings of interiors. Noticing his curiosity, she explained, "These plans are for one of my clients. I forgot them this morning and we're meeting at the store in fifteen minutes."

This was a perfect opportunity to ask if she was accepting new clients. Maybe she could make Gavin's house look as good as hers did.

But was it smart to hire his next-door neighbor? Especially when Gavin had already decided that he wanted to be friendly, but not *too* friendly?

His watch began to beep. Perfect timing. He pushed the button to silence the alarm. "I have to pick up my daughter from school."

"And I have to get back to the store."

He nodded. "Thanks again for the lasagna."

Closing the door behind himself, he started off in such a hurry that he almost tripped over a loose board. He regained his balance, and then noticed a piece of creamy paper trapped under the board. It was a wedding invitation.

With Allison's name front and center.

Gavin had a strange reaction to the news that she was getting married in four weeks. It was like…disappointment.

Which wasn't especially rational, considering his lack of interest in the woman.

TORY SEEMED FINE when Gavin met her at the classroom door, but by the time they got home she was in tears.

"I don't want to go back there." She set her mouth in a pout that looked more sad than willful.

Tory wasn't a child who cried a lot. Even as a

baby she'd been content to let her twin sister make all their demands. It was always Samantha's cry that signaled the need for a feeding, a diaper change or a desire to play or be cuddled.

"Don't you like your teacher?" Ms. Carter had seemed cheerful and kind to Gavin.

Tory shrugged.

"Weren't the other kids friendly?"

She shrugged again.

Gavin rubbed the stubble on the side of his face, feeling a little lost. Why was it so hard to communicate with his own child? Maybe if their home was a little more comfortable…

He looked around the maze of boxes for a place to sit. He could barely see the sofa, let alone relax on it. Tomorrow he really needed to make a bigger dent in the unpacking. In the meantime, he and Tory had to get out of here.

"Let's go for a walk. We'll head downtown and grab a bite to eat."

Once they were outside, he tried to raise the subject of school again, but Tory was more interested in collecting rocks than in talking. They stopped at the drugstore to buy school supplies she needed, and then moved on to the Apple Pie Café.

Gavin made a halfhearted effort to let Tory

choose from the menu, but when that didn't work, he ordered burgers and shakes for both of them.

He waited until the server left to broach the topic one more time. "Tory, you want to learn to read and write, don't you?"

She nodded.

"And you want to make friends, too. Right?"

She looked more uncertain about this.

"You *do* want to make friends," he assured her. "That's what Sam would want you to do."

Tears filled Tory's eyes again, and Gavin wondered if mentioning her sister had been the wrong thing to do.

The server returned with their food and Gavin opened Tory's burger to take out the pickle. If Sam had been here, he'd have given her Tory's pickle and his, too. But he shouldn't think about that. Shouldn't look at Tory and imagine another little girl sitting right beside her…

Double trouble. That's what his brother Matthew had called them, though always with a smile. He'd been a rock of support to Gavin in those first years after Marianne had left, always finding time to call or visit despite the demands of his job and his own family.

Then, again, after Sam's death, Matthew had

been the one person who had really seemed to understand what he was going through. He'd leaned on Matt a lot. Too much, perhaps. It had never occurred to him that maybe his brother needed a little support, too.

But plowing through each day and helping Tory get through hers had been about all he could manage.

Gavin left the subject alone after that. He was glad to see that despite her unhappiness about school, there was nothing wrong with Tory's appetite. The first while after Sam's accident she hadn't eaten much, and Gavin still felt she had some catching up to do.

After they'd finished their meal and settled the bill, they started for home. Tory paused at one of the store windows along the way.

It was Allison Bennett's shop, The Perfect Thing.

The sofa in the display window invited customers to come inside and get comfortable. Blankets and pillows had been artfully arranged around a tray holding a pretty teapot and two china mugs.

As she'd done in her own home, in this window Allison had created a heartwarming sense of "home." The exact kind of home he intended to design himself, now that he was starting his own business.

The exact kind of home he wanted to live in, as well.

"Can we go inside, Daddy?"

He was curious to see more, too.

A bell chimed as he opened the door. A well-dressed woman in her forties stood at a table in the back, flipping through a book of fabric samples. Though he couldn't see Allison, he could hear her speaking. "I think I've got just the thing. Hang on a minute."

Tory spotted a cabinet filled with miniature figurines of people, animals and birds. She squealed with pleasure. "Can I look, Daddy?"

He went to the cabinet with her, noting the ones she seemed to like the most. Her birthday was in October. The miniatures would make a terrific gift.

"These are more expensive," Allison said, "but just feel them. Pure raw silk. Scrumptious." She stepped into his line of vision as she set another heavy book of samples before her customer. "If you want to take these home to see them in your bedroom, you can sign them out."

She glanced up and the moment she spotted him her spine stiffened and her cheeks turned pink.

He smiled. "My daughter is fascinated by your miniatures."

"Is Tory here?" She went over to the cabinet. "Hi, Tory. Let me unlock this for you."

Allison's customer in the back decided she wanted to borrow both fabric books and so Allison left Tory with the figurines as she made a note of the woman's name and the books she'd taken. When she came back to Tory, she removed a figurine of a woman in Victorian dress from the cabinet.

"This one's my favorite. Isn't she beautiful?"

Gavin left the two of them to talk and wandered farther into the shop, drawn by the unique merchandise and the clever displays. Every time he doubled back, he discovered something new.

Several things here would look great at home, he thought. That mirror. The blue-and-red rug. A leather ottoman. At least he thought they would look great. He didn't entirely trust his own instincts on this. Though he had a good eye for design, soft furnishings had never held much interest for him.

As he browsed, he could hear the murmur of Allison and Tory's conversation. He was astonished by how much his daughter had to say. She'd barely looked at Allison when they'd met on moving day, and it usually took her a long time to warm up to strangers.

Finally, he had to interrupt. "We should be getting home, Tory." Allison looked up at him. She had cat's eyes, green and curious. "I hope we didn't take up too much of your time."

"Absolutely not. It's been fun." Allison locked the cabinet with an old-fashioned brass key. He focused on her hands, small and delicate, with long fingers and nicely kept nails. The real kind, not the shiny fake ones with white tips that the women in his office back in Hartford had favored.

Tory said goodbye and thanks, without any prompting from her father. It was only as they were walking along the sidewalk toward home that one little detail struck him.

Allison hadn't been wearing an engagement ring.

CHAPTER THREE

THE WEEK FELT LONG to Allison. She thought about her new neighbors often, but she hadn't seen them since their impromptu visit to her shop on Monday. Twice, she had had dinner with her father, and then she spent a couple of evenings sorting out her fall inventory, and finally it was Friday.

She closed her shop at six o'clock sharp. It had been a slow day, and she told herself to be thankful for that. In a couple of weeks, when the leaves started changing, tourists would flock to the area and she'd be busy enough. Just as she was about to head for home, her friend Sandy called.

"So, how are things going?"

Allison knew that Sandy meant well, but the sympathy in her tone was annoying. She purposefully made her voice upbeat and happy. "Fine. Everything's great."

"Got plans for tonight?"

Though she'd been looking forward to her evening alone, Allison hated to admit it. "No."

"I could arrange a last-minute potluck at our place. Daniel has this friend I've been wanting to introduce to you."

"Friend?"

"A guy, actually. Barry. He just split with his wife and…"

"No, thanks." The matchmaking had begun. Allison had known it would be only a matter of time. "I'm not ready to start meeting new guys."

"Are you sure?"

There was something in Sandy's voice that hinted at facts that remained unspoken. "Why?"

"Tyler's already met someone. They're going out tonight. Gosh, Allison, I didn't want to be the one to tell you."

"It's okay. Really." And it was. "I hope he has a good time."

"You could come for dinner, anyway. I don't have to invite Barry."

"Thanks, Sandy, but it's been a busy week at work." Sort of. "And I have a lot of catching up to do at home."

Once Sandy had accepted that she really was

okay, that she wouldn't be going home and crying her eyes out, Allison was able to leave the shop.

She wasn't sure why she'd declined the invitation, when actually she was ready to start dating. It was just that the guy had to be someone special. He had to be...

"Oh, sorry!" As she rounded the corner to Robin Crescent, she almost tripped over Tory on her tricycle. Her father, hovering a foot or two behind her, apologized on his daughter's behalf.

"We shouldn't have been going so fast."

"You weren't," she assured him. "It was the hedge. It blocked my view."

He'd put a hand on Tory's handlebars and now he steered her to the far side of the walk. He was a protective dad, Gavin Gray.

Also...kind of sexy.

He was wearing jeans and a white T-shirt that showed off nice broad shoulders and a flat stomach. And why was she noticing?

She transferred her attention to his smiling daughter. Since showing her the miniatures, the little girl had warmed up considerably.

"Hi, Tory. It's a great night for a bike ride. Having fun?"

"Yes."

"How was the first week of school?" She knew she'd asked the wrong question when Tory's smile faded instantly.

"It takes a while to get used to a new place and new people," Gavin said diplomatically. "But we should let Allison go on her way, Tory. I'm sure she has things she needs to be doing."

Allison had no things that needed doing, but she didn't correct him. Every time she met him, Gavin seemed determined to keep their relationship pleasant but distant. She could have accepted that, but there were also times when she thought she read something else in his eyes.

Interest. Attraction.

Or was that just wishful thinking on her part?

She said goodbye and went home to leftovers from her most recent dinner with her father. Less than an hour later, as she was contemplating her television options for the evening, she heard a knock at the door.

She was surprised to find Tory on her porch.

"Hi." The little girl's expression was expectant.

"Hi, Tory. Where's your dad?"

"Talking on the phone." Tory looked past

her. "Do you have any of those toys you had at the store?"

"I do have a cool collection of salt and pepper shakers, but I'd better talk to your father first. Does he know where you are?"

She'd only just asked the question when she heard Gavin's voice calling from next door. "Tory? Are you out here?"

Allison stepped out to the porch and waved at him. "She's at my place."

"Thank God." He dashed over, shaking his head. "Tory, what are you doing? You're not supposed to leave the house without telling me."

"I didn't cross the street, Daddy."

He closed his eyes. Took a deep breath. A fine sheen of moisture was visible on his forehead. Allison wouldn't have blamed him for being upset, but he seemed more than that.

He took another breath. "Sorry for the interruption, Allison. Tory, we'd better go home and review a few rules before we watch our movie."

"But Allison has something to show me."

"Allison's busy."

Seeing the little girl's face begin to crumple, Allison felt that she had to speak up. "She could stay for a while, if that's okay with you."

"But I'm sure you and your fiancé have plans."

His assumption startled her. "Did someone tell you I was engaged?"

"I saw a wedding invitation on your porch. I'm sorry. I shouldn't have read it."

"No problem. But actually my fiancé and I recently split up. The invitations were delivered because I forgot to cancel with the printer."

"Oh." He looked at her speculatively, before assuming a polite, neutral expression again. "I'm sorry to hear that."

Tired of sympathy, she purposefully misunderstood him. "It wasn't a large order. We had planned on a small wedding."

"I didn't mean about the printer." His eyes sparkled, amused.

"The broken engagement part is okay, too. Better to figure it out now than later."

"If it didn't feel right, then, yes."

She paused, wondering what his story was. She'd assumed he was divorced, but she'd seen no indication that he shared custody with Tory's mother.

So maybe he was widowed.

"Can I see the toys now?" Tory was tired of a conversation that she couldn't really follow.

"Tory, we're interrupting…."

"I was going to show her my collection of salt and pepper shakers. They're based on characters from nursery rhymes. I thought she'd get a kick out of them."

"I'm sure she would, but…"

"And then I thought we'd bake cookies," Allison added on impulse.

Tory's eyes grew round.

"Maybe another night." Gavin took his daughter's hand, but she didn't move when he tried to lead her away.

"Daddy, please?"

How could he resist that face? Allison certainly couldn't. "Really, Gavin, I'd love to have her company."

He must have seen that she was sincere, because a moment later he relented. "Fine."

Tory produced a brilliant smile.

"See that cupboard?" Allison pointed to the hutch in the dining room. "That's where I keep the salt and pepper shakers. Try and guess which nursery rhymes they match."

"Okay!" Tory dashed off and a moment later she called out, "I see Jack and Jill. And Puss in Boots."

"Good work, Tory. I'll be there in a minute to get them down for you." She smiled at Gavin. "Don't worry. We're going to have fun."

She could tell it took some effort for him to leave alone. Recalling his earlier anxiety, Allison wondered if there was a reason he was so protective.

Did it have anything to do with the missing mother?

Allison set aside her curiosity and resolved to have a good time with Tory. She let the child play with the salt and pepper shakers for a while and when she'd tired of that, they went to the kitchen to mix cookie dough.

"What kind should we make?" Allison asked.

Tory shook her head. "You pick."

"Oatmeal raisin or chocolate chip?"

"I don't care."

Assuming she was just being polite, Allison made the most obvious choice. "Well, let's do chocolate chip, then."

She was rewarded with another big smile.

THE HOUSE FELT EMPTY without his daughter. Gavin knew he ought to take advantage of the time to do some unpacking. He got as far as setting out the lawn chairs on the deck. The view was so enticing, he settled on one of them.

A couple of ducks were feeding in the grass along the lakeshore. The sinking sun cast long shadows over the water. Gavin stared into the dark patches and thought of the days when sitting and doing nothing would have horrified him. He wondered if he'd ever get his old energy back.

Time passed the way it usually did when he was in one of these moods, with his brain stuck in neutral, just like his body.

Life was less painful this way.

At some point, the phone began to ring. He wanted to ignore it, but knowing it might be Tory, he hurried inside.

The number on display was a familiar legal firm in Hartford. "Matt?"

"Hey, bro. How's the new place?"

Gavin perched on one of his many moving cartons. "Fine. How are things with you?"

"Don't ask."

"It's kind of late to be at the office, isn't it?"

His brother sighed. "Like I said, don't ask."

"Is it a new case?"

Matthew didn't reply.

Just screw it for once, Gavin wanted to say.

No matter how important work seems to you right now, your family is more important. Go home. Be with them.

"Say hi to Gillian and the kids for me. Tory and I miss you guys." That was the one bad thing about this move. They were too far away from his brothers and his mom. He and his siblings didn't always see eye-to-eye, but ever since they'd been kids, Sunday afternoons had been family time. "Have you heard from Nick lately?"

"Not for a while."

Gavin could guess why. "Must be a new girlfriend in the picture."

"It's hard to keep track," Matthew agreed. "You give Tory a hug from us. Is she really handling the move okay?"

"It's been an adjustment," Gavin admitted. "But she's taken to one of our neighbors. When Tory's around Allison, she's almost like herself again."

"That's great. Are they in the same grade?"

"Um, no. Allison's an adult."

"An adult, huh? Older?"

"A few years younger than me, I'd guess."

"And pretty? Unattached?"

It was his turn to say, "Don't ask."

Matthew laughed. "Okay, I won't. But I have a feeling I'll be hearing that name again soon."

"Don't get your hopes up." Remembering Allison's warm smile and her curious green eyes, Gavin thought maybe it was advice he should be giving himself.

TORY HAD NEVER MADE COOKIES before, and she was eager to help. As Allison slid the first batch into the oven, the young girl settled on a stool so she could keep an eye on them through the oven door.

"This is fun."

Allison opened the dishwasher and loaded the dirty dishes. "What's your favorite part?"

"Adding the chocolate chips."

"I thought you were going to say licking the beaters."

"That was good, too."

She was so easy to please. Allison grinned, thinking she hadn't enjoyed herself this much on a Friday night in ages. And that included when things had been going well between her and Tyler.

Seven minutes later, the timer rang and Allison pulled out the first tray of cookies. She put two on a plate for Tory and poured her a glass of milk.

"Allison?" Tory's mouth was smeared with chocolate. "Do you have a sister?"

"No. I'm an only child like you." Allison could tell right away that she'd said something wrong. "What is it, Tory? Have I made you sad?"

"I had a sister."

Had. The word hit her like a solid punch. She tried to catch her breath. "Did you?"

"Sam was supposed to hold Daddy's hand like me, but she ran away. She wanted to pet the dog. But she didn't see the motorcycle."

Allison froze. It sounded as if Tory's sister had been in an accident, and she was terrified of saying the wrong thing. No wonder Gavin had freaked out when Tory disappeared. The poor man.

"I'm so sorry." She stroked Tory's shoulder. Her impulse was to change the subject, but Tory must be talking about this because she wanted to. Maybe she even *needed* to. "How old was your sister?"

"Same as me."

"You were twins? Oh, honey. You must miss your sister so much."

"Sam liked cookies. She liked chocolate chips the best."

Allison drew in a shaky breath. This was okay. Tory wasn't falling apart. She couldn't, either. "What do *you* like the best?"

Before the little girl could answer, the door-bell rang.

"That's prob'ly my dad." The smile on Tory's face said everything about her feelings for her father. She slid off the stool and ran for the front door.

Allison waited in the kitchen. She felt awkward facing Gavin after Tory's revelations. No wonder he looked so tired and sad all the time. What did you say to someone who had lost a child? What could you possibly say?

CHAPTER FOUR

As soon as he saw his daughter, Gavin felt better. Tory's mouth and hands were smeared with chocolate. She actually looked happy. "We made chocolate chips, Daddy."

"Is that why it smells so great in here?"

"Sorry I couldn't get to the door," Allison called from the back of the house. "Come on through to the kitchen."

He swung Tory up onto his shoulders, then followed the sound of Allison's voice. Her house was a lot smaller than his and it only took a few steps to arrive in the kitchen, where Allison was removing a tray from the oven. She slid the hot cookies onto wire racks, then nodded toward a previous batch.

"Help yourself."

She glanced at him for only an instant, but it was long enough for him to realize that somehow she knew about Samantha. He'd seen that look, a mixture of kindness and sorrow and discomfort, too often not to recognize it. Tory must have said something.

He took her up on the offer of a cookie, but didn't taste a thing as he bit into it. Hoping to distract himself, he checked out the room.

It was decorated in French country style. The focal point was an amazing copper hood over a stove that looked as if it belonged to another era. The counters were butcher block and a beautiful cream farmhouse sink was inlaid into the surface.

A kitchen like this would be perfect for the cottage he was designing right now. Not to mention for his own house.

Should he reconsider hiring Allison to help with the decorating? "Your kitchen is beautiful."

"Thanks. I redid it when I bought the place."

"Did you do all the design work yourself?"

She nodded.

"Our kitchen could use some freshening up. In fact, the whole house is in need of paint, window coverings and carpets."

"If you're thinking of hiring someone to consult on the project, I'd be glad to show you my portfolio." She hesitated, seeming to sense his reluctance. "Or I can recommend someone from North Conway if you'd prefer."

"If I was going to hire anyone, it would be you." But he still wasn't sure where he wanted to draw the line with his neighbor. Tory liked her, he liked her… But somehow this all seemed too easy. "I wouldn't want to impose. You seemed busy at the store."

"Actually, I have some spare time in my schedule since I just canceled a three-week holiday."

For the wedding and the honeymoon, he realized. He wondered what had happened to make them call off the wedding. Was Allison heartbroken about it? If so, she was doing a good job of hiding her pain.

"Will you make my room pretty?" Tory asked from her perch on his shoulders. "Daddy said we were going to paint it."

"I'd love to help you with that, Tory." As if sensing Gavin's doubts, she added, "You wouldn't have to pay me. I'd do it for fun."

"Of course I'll pay you." He realized he was committed now. And maybe it was for the best. He hadn't even managed to unpack on his own.

"Well, squirt." He pulled on Tory's legs. "I think it's time we started that movie."

"Can we watch it here?"

He didn't blame Tory for wanting to stay. He did, too. "Allison's probably seen *Mary Poppins* before."

"That's always fun to watch. Why don't you bring the movie over? I'll make popcorn."

Popcorn was the final straw. "Pleeease, Daddy?" Tory pleaded, and Gavin couldn't resist.

"Okay. I'll run home and get the DVD." He lifted Tory off his shoulders and settled her on a stool. By the time he returned, Allison was scooping popcorn into three paper bags with Tory's help.

"Just like the theater, Daddy."

Allison's family room was wonderfully cozy for watching movies, with an overstuffed sofa and lots of cushions and blankets. Gavin was reminded of the show window at her store.

"Can I sit in the middle?" Tory plopped herself onto one of the down-stuffed cushions, and he and Allison settled themselves on either side.

By the time she'd finished her popcorn, though, Tory was getting sleepy. She settled her head on a pillow on her father's lap and Allison covered her with a light blanket.

The movie was only half over when Tory fell asleep. Gavin stroked her fine hair, then smiled at Allison. "She's down for the count."

Allison looked at him solemnly. In her eyes he saw the same compassion he'd glimpsed earlier. "Tory told me about her sister today. I'm really sorry, Gavin."

He was relieved she knew. And glad he hadn't been the one to have to tell her. "It's been hard on her."

"She told me they were twins."

"Yeah. Samantha was the firstborn. It really seemed to make a difference with their personalities. From day one, Sam led the way for her sister. Tory's been lost without her."

"There was a set of twins in my grade at school, and they were amazingly close."

"That was Sam and Tory. Sam was very protective. She seemed to know what her sister wanted better than Tory knew herself."

"Is that why Tory's so hesitant about decisions? I thought she was just shy."

"She wasn't acting shy tonight." He couldn't remember the last time he'd seen his daughter so enthusiastic, so happy, so...*alive.*

"That's true."

"I'm sorry we took over your evening."

"It's been great. Honestly. Tory's a real sweetie."

"It's been a while since I've seen her this happy," Gavin admitted. "Even before Sam's accident, she was the quiet one. Maybe things would have been different if she'd had her mother."

He wondered if Marianne had any idea of the gaping hole she'd left behind. If she could see how much Tory was hurting now, surely she'd want to be here.

"Was their mother in the accident, too?"

"No. She left long ago."

"Left?"

"Yeah." He was surprised to discover that he actually wanted to tell her more, but Tory stirred just then. She stretched out her arms and yawned. "Is the movie over, Daddy?"

The DVD had continued to play, though Gavin and Allison hadn't paid much attention to it. Gavin hit the stop button on the remote control. "It's over for tonight. Come on, sweetheart. We need to get you to bed."

He sat up and scooped his daughter into his arms. She snuggled her face against his chest and he kissed the top of her head. She smelled like popcorn and chocolate-chip cookies.

He noticed Allison watching them, a tentative smile on her face.

"Hand me your keys," she said. "I'll get the front door for you." A plate of cookies she'd covered with plastic wrap was waiting in the kitchen and she took that, too, leaving her own house unlocked as she accompanied them across the lawn.

The night was still and quiet, and the cool air, hinting at autumn, was a surprise. Gavin held Tory closer to his chest and walked briskly. Allison unlocked their front door, pushing it wide open, then stepping inside after they'd paused to turn on the lights.

"Thanks. I'll be right back." He carried Tory up the stairs to her room, where he settled her into bed.

"Daddy…" she began, but she fell asleep before she could finish whatever it was she was going to say.

He stared at her for a few seconds, his heart filled with love for the fragile creature in his care. A parent's first job was to keep his children safe, and he'd failed with Sam.

He had to do better for Tory.

Allison wasn't sure if Gavin expected her to go or stay. She closed the door and decided to give him a few minutes, anyway. Glancing around, she was surprised to see so many boxes stacked against the walls.

They'd been here for over a week. Why was it taking so long to get settled?

Maybe the task was overwhelming. Despite all the previous owners, not much had changed since the McLaughlins had lived here. The house desperately needed paint and new flooring. Allison hoped Gavin was serious about letting her help. Whether she was paid or not, it didn't matter to her. She'd love to get her hands on this place.

"Sorry to keep you waiting." Gavin was back. He noticed her scrutiny and shrugged apologetically. "It's a mess, I know. I just can't seem to motivate myself to deal with it."

"Moving is always tough. It must be even harder when you have a young child." And if you were depressed over the loss of another child.

She wanted to go back to what they'd been talking about earlier. The twins' mother. Why had she left? Was she in touch, at all?

"That's a good excuse. But I could be making better use of my time."

"Well, if you were serious about letting me

help you, I'd be glad to do it. I've always loved this house. I had a…" She paused. "A friend who used to live here."

"Really? Who was your friend?" It was too dark to see Gavin's face clearly. But he definitely sounded interested.

"Her name was Marianne McLaughlin."

Gavin went still and silent. Had she said something wrong?

"You and Marianne McLaughlin were friends?" he finally asked, slowly, as if it were some unbelievable thing.

"Sometimes it felt more like enemies, but yes. We were in the same grade. Anyway, the point is, I know this house. Marianne had the run of the place when she was growing up, and we spent a lot of time here."

She laughed, but Gavin didn't join in.

"I'd been meaning to ask if you happened to know her."

"Why—do you know Marianne, too?" Her good mood evaporated. Suddenly she felt a chill, as if a ghost had just brushed past her. She had a flashback to her childhood, to the feeling she'd get whenever Marianne took something of hers. It had happened a lot.

"Yeah. I knew Marianne, all right." Gavin went to the kitchen and opened the high cupboard above the sink. Pulling out a bottle of scotch, he poured himself a glass, then looked at her inquiringly.

She shook her head no.

He downed his drink in one swallow, then looked at her again. "Marianne is the mother of my twins."

CHAPTER FIVE

"MAYBE I'LL HAVE that drink after all," Allison said.

Gavin pulled down the bottle again. "Did I shock you?"

"Frankly, I'm a little surprised. Yes."

"She didn't tell you about us," he guessed. "Or maybe you haven't seen her in a while?"

"Right on both counts."

"Ice?" When she nodded he tried to make it to the fridge, but tripped over a box. He swore, then moved around it. "Let's go out to the deck," he suggested. "It's the only place that isn't a complete shambles around here."

Gingerly, she followed him to the patio doors. A couple of recliners and some deck chairs were arranged to take advantage of the view, though it was too dark to see much at the moment. She walked past these to the railing, where she leaned out to face the lake.

Moonlight gilded the rippled water and she could just make out the diving dock where she and Marianne had sunbathed and swam for hours on end. Those were some of the happiest times she had had with Marianne. She only wished there had been more of them.

For some reason, Marianne had seemed to get a kick out of winning things that Allison wanted. It didn't matter if it was an art competition or a boyfriend.

"I can't believe Marianne is a mother."

"Why do you say that?" Gavin turned on an outdoor heater, then offered her a chair beside it. There was just enough light so that she could make out the line of his jaw, the solid breadth of his shoulders.

She turned away from the sight. Right now, she couldn't handle being attracted to him. *He and Marianne had had two children together. Gavin Gray and Marianne.* It was a picture she didn't want to contemplate.

"I'm just confused. I didn't know Marianne was married." She swirled the ice cubes in her glass, fighting a sudden impulse to down the drink in one long swallow.

He was quiet for a while, then said, "We were

never married. We'd only been seeing each other a short time when she found out she was pregnant."

Strangely, Allison felt relieved to hear they hadn't been married. At the same time, she was still shocked about the pregnancy. She only heard from Marianne once or twice a year, but you'd think she might have mentioned that she was having twins.

"I can't help feeling we're talking about different women."

"Could there be two Marianne McLaughlins in New England? Both from Squam Lake?"

Now Allison sighed. "I guess it's the same woman. But if Marianne is Tory's mom, then where is she? You said she left you years ago, but why?"

"She walked out when the twins were just one year old. And as for why she did it…" He shrugged. "Your guess is as good as mine."

But mothers didn't just leave their children for no reason. Marianne, for all her faults, wouldn't have, either. Would she?

"Are you sure she didn't give a reason?"

"Maybe there were signs I didn't see. I don't know. But when I say she walked out on us, that's literally what happened. She said she was going away for a girls' weekend. She never came back."

"Did you question her friends?"

"That's the funny part. She didn't have any friends. At least none that I'd ever met or heard her mention. She never showed any interest in meeting the people I worked with, and she didn't seem keen to get to know the neighbors, either. That's why I was so glad when she said she wanted a weekend away. I thought finally she'd met some women she liked."

The profile he presented fit Allison's memories of Marianne perfectly. "She was the same at school. The guys all liked her, but she didn't really have friends."

"Except for you."

"Except for me," she agreed. For some reason Marianne had chosen Allison as the one person she could tolerate, starting in kindergarten when they'd both gravitated to the craft table. After that, they'd taken art classes together all the way through their senior year.

That common interest had come to haunt Allison, though. She wasn't very old before she'd realized that although she was good with color and artful arrangements, Marianne was the one with the real talent. An original spirit was what their high school art teacher had called her.

How Marianne had lorded that one over Allison.

Many times Marianne's friendship had been a burden that Allison gladly would have shed. Her spitefulness had caused all sorts of problems with the other kids in their class. But whenever Allison complained to her parents, her father would be quite stern. He'd point out that Marianne didn't have a father to guide her, the way she did, and he'd urged her to be patient and understanding.

The fact that Marianne didn't have a father hadn't seemed like much of an excuse to Allison. There was another kid in their class who was missing one of his parents, and Scott wasn't a jerk just because he didn't have a mother.

But Allison liked pleasing her father, and so she'd stuck by Marianne over the years. Even when her other friends called her a fool.

"Well, whether Marianne had girlfriends or not," Gavin continued, "she didn't come home that night. Or any other night after that."

"So you haven't heard from her in all those years?"

"Not a word."

She considered the various implications. "Do you think she knows about what happened to Samantha?"

"Not unless she was still in Hartford at the time and read about it in the local papers."

"She wasn't. She's been living in the White Mountains for quite a while now." Allison wondered if Gavin was disappointed to hear that. "Were you hoping to find her in Squam Lake?"

"Not at all."

"It's not why you moved here?"

"I wanted out of the rat race of the city."

"There are lots of other small towns in New England."

Finally, he conceded the point. "I suppose I chose this one because of the ties to Tory's mother. I thought maybe I'd find someone who knew Marianne. Who could help me locate her."

"In other words...someone like me." She found herself resenting the hopeful look he gave her. She and Gavin had been working their way toward friendship, and now—suddenly—Marianne was part of the picture. And she didn't want Marianne in the picture. Marianne had always changed everything.

"You had to know that moving here was a long shot," she added. "Why not hire a private investigator to track her down?"

"I considered that, but my brothers talked me out of it."

"You have more than one?"

He held up two fingers. "Matt's a lawyer and Nick is a cop—they both live in Hartford. Neither one of them cared much for Marianne."

Which showed that they had good taste. Allison wrinkled her nose, aware that her thoughts were bitter. Marianne had always been able to bring out her dark side.

"So you let it drop."

"It wasn't until Samantha died that finding Marianne seemed imperative. Then, as luck would have it, I stumbled across an old box of her belongings in the attic. Inside were some school papers, including her high school diploma. That's how I found out she'd grown up in Squam Lake."

"And you decided to move here."

"I needed to do something. Tory was depressed. We both were. Too many memories in that house. In Hartford, for that matter."

"I can imagine." He had her sympathy now. Losing Marianne was one thing, but losing a young daughter was something else entirely.

"I'd already been thinking about moving. I wanted a small town. Something not too far from my family. Squam Lake seemed like the right answer on several levels."

What he said seemed sort of reasonable. Except… "You went so far as to buy Marianne's old house." That was just a little *too* creepy for Allison. It was one thing to want to find your daughter's mother, but it was another to be obsessed by the idea.

"That part was coincidence. I couldn't believe it when our real-estate agent said the house used to belong to the McLaughlin family. I figured it was a sign."

And maybe it was, Allison thought. For Gavin, it was a sign that he was getting closer to the mother of his babies. For her, it was a sign that she'd better not get too close to a man obsessed with another woman.

GAVIN COULDN'T BELIEVE that he'd finally found a link to Marianne. Though Allison didn't seem to have liked her that much, she'd actually been Marianne's friend. There was something ironic about that, but at the moment he needed to focus on other things.

"Allison?"

"Yes?"

He'd given her an opportunity to ask her questions. Now it was his turn. "Have you heard from Marianne lately?"

"The last time was about a year ago."

He waited, but she didn't offer him any more than that. He could tell she didn't want to talk about Marianne any longer, but he couldn't let this drop. "Do you have a phone number or an e-mail address?" he pressed.

"When she gets in touch, it's usually by e-mail. I can give you the last address she used, but it probably won't help. She lives in a trailer with no Internet access and doesn't get to town often."

In the dim light of the moon, Gavin tried to read Allison's expression. Was Marianne really that reclusive? "I can't imagine Marianne in a trailer."

"How well did you know her?"

It was a valid question. "I'm beginning to realize, not that well."

There was a long silence. Then, almost reluctantly, Allison asked, "How did you two meet?"

He hadn't thought about that night in years. "It was at an evening reception at an art gallery in Hartford. I can't remember the name of the artist. The paintings were different. Not my taste at all."

But though he'd gone to the show hoping to find a gift for his mother's new condominium and had been disappointed in that respect, the evening hadn't been a total waste. He'd been about to leave when a beautiful woman had offered him a glass of wine and then introduced herself as Marianne McLaughlin.

Within half an hour he was totally bewitched.

They had an intense four-week affair. And by the beginning of the fifth week, while he was haunting jewelry stores looking for the perfect ring to tempt her, she was already drifting away.

He'd tried to deny what was happening. Found excuses to explain why she was slow returning his calls. Why suddenly she could only find time for him once or twice a week, rather than every night like before.

By the sixth week, he was finally getting the picture. He returned the ring and considered breaking off the relationship completely, rather than dealing with Marianne's hot-and-cold routine.

Then Marianne had emerged from the washroom at his condo with a strip of plastic in her hands.

"I'm pregnant," she'd said, her face devoid

of color. And both of their lives had been changed forever.

Wood creaked as Allison shifted in her chair. "So Marianne would have been about twenty-two when you met?"

"Yes. She was twenty-three by the time the babies were born, though."

"What was their birthdate?"

"October eighteenth." He could see Allison thinking, probably trying to remember if she'd heard anything from her friend around that time. He wondered if she wanted to corroborate his story or refute it.

At any rate, clearly she came up with nothing. She shook her head, her expression rueful. "That's just so hard to imagine. Marianne never said *anything* about being pregnant or having children."

If someone had told him this story out of the blue, he would have had difficulty accepting it, too. His firsthand experiences with Marianne, however, had made it all too real for him.

"In the weeks after the babies were born, Marianne was tired and irritable. She refused even to hold them until they were several weeks old."

"Postpartum depression?"

"That's what I thought. I took her to the doctor and she was given a prescription, but it didn't seem to help." Much as he'd hoped that Marianne would bond with their babies eventually, it just hadn't happened. Marianne had told him she didn't want children, and clearly she'd meant it.

When they'd first found out about the pregnancy, he'd tried to reassure her. "It'll be okay. We'll get married and move into a nice house. I have some savings. You won't need to work."

"But what if I want to work?"

"Well, sure, if you want to." Oddly, he didn't know what Marianne did for a living. When they'd been dating, she'd left her apartment every day at eight in the morning and often didn't return until late, but he had no idea where she went or what she did when they were apart. When he asked her questions, she accused him of being controlling.

"I can't do this," she'd said. "We have to get rid of it."

"You mean have an abortion? No way, Marianne. No way." He still didn't know how he'd talked her out of terminating the pregnancy, especially once she'd found out she was carrying twins, but he was so glad that he had. He couldn't imagine what his life would have been like without Tory and Sam. Even having Sam for only five years was better than never having her at all.

"This is quite a story, Gavin."

"Maybe to you." His jaw tightened. "It's more than a story to me and to Tory."

He heard Allison's quick intake of breath and turned in time to see compassion soften her features.

"I apologize for sounding heartless."

"You didn't. It's just a sensitive subject with me." Alison didn't have it in her to be heartless. Watching her with Tory tonight had given Gavin the strangest, warmest feeling inside.

There was something so likable about his new neighbor. And now, in the moonlight, she looked even prettier than she did by day. Gavin was surprised by the urge he felt to kiss her.

The impulse was insane and the timing even more so. Since Marianne had left him he hadn't been interested in any other woman, and yet he couldn't deny that he was attracted to this new neighbor of his.

He got out of his chair and went over to the railing. His life was too crazy as it was for him to be feeling this way. Especially about the one person he'd found who might have a connection to Marianne.

"Will you leave Squam Lake if you don't find her?"

He considered the question. "I hadn't thought that far ahead, but no. I don't think we'll leave." He angled his head to see her more clearly. "Is there some reason why you think I won't find her?"

"No," Allison said, turning away.

Gavin wondered why she was uncomfortable with the idea of him finding Marianne. Was it because of old loyalties to her friend?

"I guess what I'm wondering," Allison continued, "is why it's so important to you."

The answer was obvious to him.

"For Tory."

"Are you sure? If Marianne left when the babies were one, Tory probably can't remember her."

"Maybe not. But children need their mothers."

"In some cases, don't you think just having a father may be enough?"

"I wish that were true." He kept his gaze on the lake, fighting to control his emotions. If he *was* enough for Tory, then she wouldn't still need to be seeing a counselor, would she?

"From what I've seen, you're a terrific father. And Tory is a wonderful girl. If Marianne chose to walk out of her children's lives, then she's the biggest loser."

That was what his brothers were always telling him. But Gavin was almost certain they were wrong. Six years ago he hadn't been able to understand why Marianne had deserted their kids. Now, he was sure that if she knew what had happened to Sam, she would regret that decision. That she would want to make up for lost time with Tory.

Her brother and Allison obviously disagreed, but Gavin knew he had to find Marianne and give her that chance.

CHAPTER SIX

WHEN HER DRINK WAS FINISHED, Allison said good-night. As she crossed the lawn between their homes, she was aware of Gavin on his own front stoop, watching until she was safely home. She turned to wave, touched by his gallant gesture.

Her house still smelled of baking, a sweet, welcoming scent. She went to the family room, where the three of them had watched the movie. She tidied the cushions, then picked up the empty popcorn bags and glasses and carried them to the kitchen.

Poor Tory. What a childhood she'd had. Abandoned by her mother. Then, the death of her twin. She'd seemed happy tonight, though, when they were baking cookies. Everyone said how resilient children were, and Allison hoped she'd be fine. One lucky thing… She had a good father.

Gavin. Allison stopped moving and closed her

eyes, her feelings so intense she hardly knew what to do. There'd been a moment when they'd been looking into each other's eyes where she'd been sure he was about to kiss her.

But maybe she had imagined his interest. They'd been talking about the mother of his children, for heaven's sake. What she hadn't imagined, in any case, was her own longing for that kiss.

That feeling worried her. How could she let herself be attracted to Gavin when he'd spent the entire evening talking about Marianne? He'd moved to Squam Lake, moved into the McLaughlins' old house. He claimed it was all for Tory's benefit, but Allison didn't buy that.

Obviously, he was still fixated on Marianne.

Allison finished putting the dirty dishes into the dishwasher, then went to her computer and opened the folder in which she kept her personal correspondence.

It wasn't just Marianne's fault that they kept in touch so irregularly. Allison wasn't the best correspondent, either. The first year she'd had an excuse. Marianne had left Squam Lake during one of the most difficult times of Allison's life.

First, her beloved grandmother had died in a

car crash. Allison had been the main beneficiary in her will, which included a proviso that she attend design school before taking over her grandmother's business. Her grandmother had always been the one who had seen Allison's talent and believed in her abilities.

But no sooner had Allison enrolled in the New England School of Art & Design and settled into residence, than her parents had announced they were separating. Out of the blue, her mother moved to New York City.

No wonder she'd lost track of Marianne then. She hadn't even had time to ask her why she was leaving or what her future plans involved. Whenever Marianne did send a brief e-mail, Allison's responses were always just as short.

She'd been busy. First with school, and then with launching her own design business and running her grandmother's store.

Allison brushed off a pang or two of guilt. Maybe she hadn't been much of a friend. Her father, she knew, wouldn't approve.

Scrolling through her saved messages, Allison stopped and opened a file named Marianne. She clicked on the oldest message, sent over a year after Marianne had left town.

Hey girl, what's happening? Married with kids yet? I've been traveling in the southwest. Loved painting in the desert. Met some new friends in Taos with an Internet connection and thought I'd get in touch. Use this address to write me back. If you want to.

Allison had replied, though only in a few sentences. If she was honest with herself the brevity had as much to do with her own reluctance to keep in touch with Marianne as it did with her lack of time.

After all those years of being tied to Marianne, it had been a relief finally to be free. Not to have to watch over her shoulder, waiting for Marianne to go after something Allison had that she'd decided she couldn't live without.

Like Allison's boyfriends. For some reason, all it had taken to make Marianne want someone was to know that Allison wanted him, too.

Which brought her squarely back to Gavin, didn't it?

Allison skipped ahead to a message she'd received the year Marianne had become pregnant.

Holed up in Hartford now. Got myself trapped in a terrible situation... You wouldn't believe it if I told you. Can't seem to paint. Need to get out of here, but not sure how to do it.

Allison read the message over several times. In one way, it seemed to fit with Gavin's story. Marianne unexpectedly had found herself pregnant with twins and felt trapped.

For the first time, she considered the possibility that Marianne might have had a good reason for leaving Gavin and their daughters. Yes, Marianne was self-centered. But so were many young children and teenagers. It was hard to believe that she could be so hard-hearted as to abandon her own children.

Plus, if Marianne had wanted an abortion, why hadn't she had one? Marianne had never let the opinions of others stop her from doing what she wanted. Gavin—as the father—obviously had a say in the decision, but Marianne would have been the first to insist that her body was her own and the decision was hers to make.

Was it possible that there was more to the story than Gavin had admitted? Could he have been abusive in some way, emotionally or physically?

But Allison had seen firsthand how gentle

Gavin was with Tory. She just didn't believe it could be an act.

As for explaining Marianne's behavior, only Marianne could do that. She'd send her an e-mail and see what happened. From past experience she didn't expect it would be answered for a while, but at least she'd know she'd made the effort.

As she sat down to compose her message, Allison thought over the past. According to Gavin, Marianne had deserted her family about six years ago. Wasn't that about the time that Marianne's mom, Adele, had died?

Maybe instead of a weekend trip with girl-friends, Marianne had actually traveled to Squam Lake for her mother's funeral then.

Allison had been at Adele McLaughlin's funeral, of course. She tried to recall the conversations she'd had with Marianne at that time. But she couldn't remember much. Marianne had been busy with arrangements related to the funeral and sorting out her mother's estate. No time for a heart-to-heart chat, which Marianne wasn't inclined to have at the best of times, anyway.

Frustrated by so many questions without

answers, Allison opened her most recent e-mail from Marianne, one she'd received about a year ago. She hit Reply and then started to type.

Hi, Marianne. How are you doing? Is the painting going well? I hope so. I sold two of your works this spring and only have a couple left in the shop. If you have some more, I'd love to see them.

This wasn't completely true. With every year that passed, Marianne's painting style grew darker. Her recent work didn't appeal much to Allison's customers. Still, she knew she'd try to sell anything Marianne had to give her, because that was what her father expected her to do.

It would be good to have a visit, too. It's been a long time. Any interest in heading back to your hometown? Let me know.

She said nothing about her own broken engagement—nothing about Gavin and Tory, either. Those subjects would have to wait for a face-to-face meeting.

She felt relieved as soon as the message was sent. She'd done her bit. Now she would wait to see if Marianne replied.

ALLISON ARRANGED her staffing schedule so that she had alternate weekends off. This happened to be her free weekend, so on Saturday morning she drove downtown to pick out paint samples and fabric swatches for Tory's room.

Back at home she constructed three design boards, each with a unique color and decorating theme. She'd show these to Tory, to get an idea of what she liked. The child had been through a lot in her short life and Allison was determined to design the bedroom of her dreams.

Her father called just as she was preparing to head over to the Grays'.

"I saw Tyler last night," he announced after a quick hello. "He was at the Rusty Nail with a new woman. I'm told she's an elementary schoolteacher."

"That's nice, Dad." She sat at her desk and idly shifted her computer mouse. She was afraid this call wasn't going to be short.

"Nice? I would have thought you'd be upset that he was seeing someone so soon after the breakup."

"Why would I be upset? I'm the one who gave him back his ring, remember?" She closed the document she'd been working on earlier. Her screen saver popped up.

"But are you sure you did the right thing? If you want him back, you'll have to act quickly. I don't want to hurt your feelings, but this new girl is very pretty and he seemed quite taken with her."

"My feelings aren't hurt," she assured him. And they weren't. She was absolutely fine with Tyler dating someone else. She opened her e-mail. *Receiving mail,* her computer told her.

"Are you sure?"

"Yes, Dad." She swiveled her chair to look out the window. She could just see the corner of Gavin's house from here. She thought about that moment on the deck with Gavin the night before, the zap of awareness that had passed between them. She wouldn't have felt that if she was meant to be with Tyler. "He isn't the right guy for me."

"Will you still think that a year from now, when you're all alone and Tyler and this new girl are setting up house together?"

"They've only had one date. It's a little early to predict they're going to move in together. Besides, even if I'm still unattached a year from now, what makes you think I'll be lonely? Are *you* lonely?"

"It's different for men."

"Why?"

"It just is."

"So you're not lonely?"

"Of course not."

Was he telling the truth? He did seem to have a full schedule, a lot of friends. If he dated, though, he was certainly low-key about it. He'd never introduced her to any lady friends.

"You know Gertie is about your age," she teased.

"Gertie Atwater?" Her father sounded appalled.

"She talks a lot, I know, but she has a really good heart…."

"Point made and taken." Her father sighed to indicate his resignation. "I'd better go, Allie. Talk to you later in the week, okay?"

"Sure, Dad." Allison disconnected the call, then swiveled her chair back to face her computer. *Three new messages,* the computer told her.

One of them was a bounce-back message. Her e-mail to Marianne hadn't been delivered. Allison knew she ought to feel disappointed, for Gavin's sake.

But she didn't.

GAVIN FLIPPED a slice of French toast onto his daughter's plate, then passed her the bottle of maple syrup. During the week they had cold cereal and milk for breakfast. But on the weekends he liked to make something special. French toast had always been the girls' favorite.

"Daddy?" Tory tipped the bottle over her plate and let the golden syrup spill onto the toast. She was still in her pajamas, her cheeks rosy from sleep and her dark hair flat on one side, sticking out on the other.

He snuck a kiss onto her cheek before sitting across from her. "What?"

She passed him the syrup. "Do you think Sam would've liked Allison?"

The question caught him unawares, and he took a moment to think through his answer. Why was Tory asking this? Was she avoiding forming her own opinion? "What do you think about Allison?"

"Sam didn't like ladies who yell, but Allison doesn't yell. And she knows how to make cookies. I think Sam would have liked her."

"Probably. But why do you say Sam didn't like ladies who yell? Did you know someone like that?" Had he missed something major here? He thought back on the various babysitters he'd hired. Had one of them mistreated his daughters?

"The girl who taught us swimming used to stand on the edge of the pool and yell at us. Sam didn't like that."

He smiled with relief. "The pool is a noisy place. She probably had to raise her voice to be heard. Want another piece of French toast?"

"No, thanks." As Tory finished her last bite, the doorbell rang. She peered out the front window. "It's Allison!" Jumping from her chair, she ran to the door—making her partiality for their new neighbor abundantly clear to Gavin.

He found himself smiling as he cleared away the breakfast dishes. When Tory returned, Allison was right behind her.

Allison entered the room like a fresh breeze, her pretty hair in a ponytail and her eyes sparkling. "I hope this isn't too early, but I have some design boards I wanted Tory to see. Just to give me some direction about what she'd like to do with her room."

"You move fast." Seeing the consternation on Allison's face, he added, "Which is good." He kicked one of the moving boxes that was sitting on the floor. "As you can see, I don't."

"You unpacked all the boxes in my room, Daddy."

He tried to smooth her hair with his hand, but the bump on the right side just bounced up again. "Yeah, we got that far, at least."

He glanced back at Allison. Not only had she completed the preliminary legwork on the design project, but she was perfectly groomed, from her shiny, smooth hair to her pink-polished toenails. And here he was, still in sweats and a University of Hartford T-shirt. "You'll have to excuse our appearances. We had a lazy morning."

"I watched cartoons," Tory elaborated. "Daddy read the paper."

"I usually laze around on Saturday mornings, too," Allison confessed. "But I was so excited about Tory's room I had to get started."

He glanced at the poster-sized boards in her hands. They were covered with pictures from magazines, paint chips and fabric samples. She'd written notes on them, too, in various colored marking pens.

She noticed his interest. "Don't worry if you don't like what I have here. This is just a starting point. Besides finding out more about what Tory wants, I'll need you to set a budget. Plus, I'd like to check out the lighting in the room and get some measurements. Can we go up now?"

Tory was dancing on the spot. Obviously, she shared Allison's enthusiasm. She started to lead the way and Gavin was about to follow when the phone rang. "You two go ahead. I'll be right there."

A glance at the call display told him it was his younger brother, Nick. "Hey, stranger. How are you doing?" he asked.

"Good. Pretty good." Nick didn't sound all that happy, though. Maybe he'd had a fight with his new girlfriend.

"Things okay with…" What was her name? "…Emily?"

"Oh, yeah. That's going really well."

"What about the job? Any news?" His brother was on track to realizing his lifelong dream of becoming detective on the Hartford police department. He'd finished the training and was hoping for promotion soon.

"Not yet, but it's looking good." Nick cleared his throat. "Have you talked to Matt lately?"

"Yeah, not that long ago."

"How did he sound to you?"

"A little stressed." But that was normal for their brother. He ran on overdrive, as a matter of course. "Is something wrong?"

"I don't know. I called almost every night this week, but each time Gillian said he was at work."

"Typical Matt. Why don't you try him there?"

"Eventually I did. But, Gavin, it's not right. He shouldn't be spending all his time at the office like that. I was thinking maybe you could try talking to him?"

Gavin could tell that Nick was really worried. In all honesty, so was he. "I'll try. But you know Matt. How stubborn he can be."

"Yeah." Nick cleared his throat again. "So…how are you and Tory doing?"

"We're settling in."

"Matt tells me you've got a hot neighbor. Allison, right? Have you asked her out yet?"

"The way you guys gossip, I might as well have two sisters."

"Hey, we're looking out for your love life, bro. So, have you? Asked her out?"

"No. And I'm not going to."

"What's wrong with her?"

He couldn't think of a single thing. "She's

great. But listen to this. She used to be Marianne's best friend."

"No. Are they still in touch?" After Sam's death, Nick had tried to help Gavin find the twins' mother. He'd started a missing person's investigation, but it soon became clear that Marianne had left of her own accord.

"Not on a regular basis. Allison says Marianne moves around a lot. But she e-mails every now and then. Hopefully she'll do that soon."

"Are you sure you want to see that woman again?"

"I'm not doing this for me."

"For who then—Tory? I don't think you'll be doing the kid any favor by finding her so-called mother."

Gavin was used to his brother's cynicism, though he didn't share it. "Maybe Marianne has changed."

"Then why hasn't she contacted you? You wouldn't be hard to find. You lived in the old house in Hartford up until last month."

Gavin stopped arguing. Matt and Nick both disliked Marianne—they'd never give her any benefit of doubt. But he couldn't help thinking that if Marianne knew what had happened to Sam, she *would* change.

Gavin wasn't keen to end up sharing access to his child with her estranged mother. But he was willing to put Tory's best interests first.

CHAPTER SEVEN

THERE WERE THREE ROOMS upstairs, besides the master bedroom. One had been turned into Gavin's office. Allison caught a glimpse inside, as Tory led her down the hall to the room at the end. She saw a bank of gray filing cabinets. A drafting table with a set of drawings on top. Everything in the room was neat and tidy, which told her that the general disarray in the rest of the house wasn't typical.

"This is mine," Tory said shyly, standing on the threshold of the room that had once belonged to her mother. Allison wondered if this was another co-incidence, or if somehow Gavin could have known.

"It's beautiful, Tory." The walls were still peach—Marianne's favorite color when she was in her teens—and damaged in places from the tape she'd used to hold up pictures from her art magazines.

Tory had a bed, nightstand and chest of drawers, all of light maple. The bed had been made, though not too neatly. A box of toys at the footrest was the only sign that this was a child's room.

When Marianne had lived here, the bed had been pushed against the wall to make room for her desk and easel. Most of the time they were hanging out together, Marianne would be dabbling at some picture or another.

Sometimes she'd asked Allison to pose for her. Allison had feigned reluctance, but secretly she'd been pleased to model. Marianne never painted all of her at once. She would focus on a body part such as Allison's neck or a hand. Once she'd painted her profile and had framed the canvas for a birthday present.

That had been the last present Allison had ever received from Marianne. Two months later she'd left Squam Lake for good.

"Do you have a favorite color, Tory?"

The little girl shrugged her shoulders. "Sam liked purple."

"Do you like purple?"

Tory shrugged again. She seemed uncomfortable, as if she didn't know where to look. But

Allison had seen her glance at the design boards a few times with curiosity.

"Let's put these on the bed and see what you think of them."

One board featured restful neutral tones, another sweet pastels and the third incorporated bright colors reminiscent of mangoes and green apples.

"First impression, Tory. Which do you like the best? Don't think about it, just point."

Tory looked from one to the other, shaking her head. Finally she put her hands on her cheeks in consternation. "I can't pick."

Allison realized the child was genuinely distressed. "That's okay, honey. Don't worry." She shouldn't have put Tory on the spot like that. Not when she knew how much trouble Tory had making decisions.

Still, there had to be some way of figuring out what Tory liked.

Often when she took on a new client, Allison would ask about hobbies and interests. She looked around Tory's room, but it was too tidy to offer any hints.

"Do you have a favorite toy?"

Tory nodded.

"Can I see it?" She expected Tory to go to her toybox, but instead she opened the closet doors. There were no clothes inside. Instead, the entire space was filled by a beautiful Victorian doll-house.

"Oh, my goodness. That's so beautiful."

She sat on the floor in front of the dollhouse as Tory went through each room, showing her the tiny dolls and furniture inside. Now, Allison understood why she'd been so enthralled by the miniatures at her store. They would be perfect for Tory's dollhouse, which was stunning, with authentically reproduced details. And the colors were charming.

"Would you like your room to look like this, Tory? I don't mean exactly, but we could start by using the same colors."

Tory nodded and seemed pleased.

"White eyelet bedding, embroidered pillows, a nice window seat in the dormer… No." She changed her mind. "We should put the dollhouse in the dormer. Maybe put it on a low table for you, so it's easier to play with?"

She was trying to gauge Tory's reaction to her ideas when Gavin walked in. He went to the design boards first.

"I like this." He'd pointed to the pastels.

"Good. Because what we've decided on is sort of similar. I've been inspired by Tory's dollhouse. Did you build it?"

"With Tory's help, yes. We ordered a kit from the Internet, and then we spent all winter on it."

Therapy to deal with the loss of Samantha? It seemed like a smart strategy to her. "How would you feel about using these heritage colors for the entire house?"

"Heritage sounds good. But I don't want to sacrifice functionality or comfort for the sake of design."

"We won't," she assured him. "I've never liked the sort of rooms that look good in a magazine but are totally impractical for everyday living."

"Then I say go for it."

"And what about rugs? Tory, I bet you'd like something soft, wouldn't you?"

Tory gave one of her usual shrugs. "Can I watch cartoons?" She'd clearly had enough conversation about interior design for now.

When she left the room, Gavin asked, "Were you able to draw any decisions out of her?"

"I tried. But not too successfully. Has she always had trouble making choices?"

"That was Samantha's role. I used to find Sam's protective streak endearing. But now I see that it wasn't in Tory's best interest to be so over-shadowed by her sister."

"Eventually she'll adjust…."

"That's what the counselor in Hartford said."

She was relieved to hear they'd been to one. She'd been just about to make that suggestion. "Is Tory still seeing someone?"

"We've been referred to a psychologist in North Conway. Our first appointment with her is next week."

He didn't sound very happy about it. "You don't think the counseling is going to help?"

"It hasn't so far, has it?" His gaze skimmed past hers, resting on a framed picture of Tory and her sister.

The twins were so alike it was startling, but what really caught Allison's attention was the smile on Tory's face. It was positively joyful. "They were happy little girls."

"Once. Yeah, they were."

He looked so downtrodden, she fought an urge to put her hand on his back, maybe offer him a hug. But they didn't know each other well enough for that.

"Did you have a chance to look up that e-mail address for Marianne?" he asked.

His question grated, and she wasn't sure why. "I sent an e-mail to the last address I had for her, but it bounced back."

The look of disappointment on his face was similarly annoying. Did he really think that Marianne was going to solve all his daughter's problems?

"Tory will be herself again. You just need to give her a little more time." Allison had no idea if this was true. She just hoped it was.

ON HER WAY to pick up paint from the hardware store, Allison ran into Tyler. He was with someone, and her dad had been right—she was pretty.

Allison hesitated when she first saw him. She considered ducking into the library, whose doors she was just passing; then she figured, what the heck, she might as well get this first encounter over with. Besides, she could tell Tyler had seen her, too. His face was growing redder by the second.

They smiled awkwardly at one another until they were close enough to speak. "Hi, Allie. This is Lisa Ward. Lisa, this is Allison Bennett."

Lisa's eyes narrowed as she realized she was being introduced to her new boyfriend's former fiancée. In a gesture that seemed instinctive, she put her hand on Tyler's arm.

Don't worry, Allison wanted to tell her. *I'm no threat to whatever you've got going on here.*

"How's your development project coming along?" Allison asked, genuinely interested. She and Tyler had gone to school together, dating off and on between the years they'd gone to college. She'd known Tyler for a significant chunk of her life, and just because she didn't want to marry him it didn't mean she had no feelings for him at all.

They simply weren't the kind of feelings she had when Gavin was close to her. That's all.

"The financing came through last week. I'm going ahead with the plans. I've been talking to a few architects already."

"That's great." Tyler had purchased a tract of land near the lake, which he intended to develop with recreational villas and condominiums. It was quite a leap for his small construction company, but he was ambitious and hardworking and Allison had no doubt he'd succeed.

"I heard a new architect moved into the McLaughlin place beside you," he said.

"Yes," she said cautiously, guessing where this was headed and not liking it at all.

"I don't suppose you have any idea how good he is?"

Now *her* face was turning red. "You mean at architecture?"

Tyler looked at her as if she was nuts. "That is what we were talking about."

"Of course." She cleared her throat. "I don't know anything about his credentials."

"I'll give him a call, anyway. It would be handy to work with someone who lived in the area."

"I believe he wants to start his own business and take on smaller projects."

"Can't hurt to talk to the fellow." Tyler shrugged philosophically.

An awkward pause developed.

"Well, then. Nice seeing you." Tyler started to move on, but stopped again. "By the way, when I saw your dad at the gas station a little while ago he mentioned something about a loose board on your porch?"

Because Lisa was standing beside him, Tyler couldn't see the look of annoyance on her face. But Allison could.

"I have someone lined up to fix that."

"You sure?"

"Absolutely. Have a nice afternoon." She waved them off, doing her best to hide her own annoyance. That father of hers. Was he ever going to give up?

GAVIN AND TORY SPENT Saturday afternoon exploring the town. They had lunch at a café overlooking the lake, then went for a stroll along Main Street. Through the window of the hardware store, Gavin saw Allison studying the paint display.

She was probably picking out colors for Tory's room. He'd forgotten to pay her a retainer earlier that morning. He should run in right now and rectify that.

"Tory…" He turned, but his daughter was no longer beside him. She'd run ahead on the sidewalk and was pointing to a beautiful parklike area on a hill across the street.

The town cemetery.

He hurried to catch up. "Tory? Are you okay?"

"Is that a cement-ery, Daddy?"

"Yes." Tory knew all about "cement-eries," as she called them. Samantha had been buried in

Hartford, next to his father, and he and Tory had gone to visit her every month before their move.

"It looks pretty."

He'd been worried that she'd be frightened or sad, but she didn't seem to be either. "Do you want to go for a walk in there?"

"Yes, please."

He took her hand as they crossed the street. The grass had just been mowed and the air was sweet. A black wrought-iron fence surrounded the grounds and the gate squeaked as he opened it. A pretty hand-tooled sign read Seven Oaks Cemetery, and sure enough, seven oak trees had been planted around the edges of the plot. Gavin and Tory walked past the trees, following a gravel path that led up and down each of the rows. Tory insisted on touching the marble markers. She tried to read the names, too, and the inscriptions beneath them. Gavin helped her as she stumbled over the words.

Partway through the second row, she asked, "Do you think Grandma and Uncle Matt and Uncle Nick will remember to visit Sam?"

He had to swallow first. "I'm sure they will."

"Good." Tory ran to the next marker. "Ad—" She stopped. "What does that say?"

"Adele McLaughlin." He'd said the name before he realized its significance. Holy cow, this was Tory's grandmother's grave. Below her name were the words *Mother and friend, dearly loved.*

He read the date, then realized with a shock that Adele had been buried around the time that Marianne had left him. Had her mother's death affected her decision, then?

It seemed likely enough that it had.

"Daddy, what does this one say?"

Tory had skipped ahead to a double grave, which turned out to belong to her great-grandparents.

There were other McLaughlins buried here, too, lots of them, and Gavin wondered who they all were and what their connections would be to his daughter. He felt a surge of anger toward Marianne. This was Tory's heritage. Marianne had no right to deprive her of this. No right at all.

At the sound of the squeaking gate, he turned. Simultaneously Tory exclaimed, "Daddy, look. It's Allison."

His daughter started to run and Allison laughed when Tory caught up to her. She took her hand and continued up the path.

"How did you find us?" Tory wanted to know.

"I was putting the paint for your room in my car when I looked up here and saw you. Hi, Gavin."

She seemed a little worried as her eye caught his. She glanced at the marker by his feet and her frown deepened. "Is everything okay?"

"Sure. We're just out for a walk."

"What color is the paint?" Tory wanted to know. Allison pulled a paint chip from her skirt pocket.

"Pretty." Tory seemed to lose interest then. She went back to running up and down the rows, no longer bothering to try to read the names.

Gavin watched, glad to see his daughter carefree for a change. At the same time, he was extremely aware of the woman at his side.

"Does she know these are her relatives?"

"No clue." He felt another rush of resentment toward Marianne. "But she should."

Allison nodded but didn't look at him. Gavin felt a prick of envy. She knew so much more about Marianne and the McLaughlin family than he did. He wished he could get her to open up on the subject.

"We've seen Marianne's mother's grave, but where is her father buried?"

"He isn't here." Allison sounded uncomfortable.

"Is he still alive?"

"Actually…I don't know. Marianne's father was never in the picture. Didn't she tell you that?"

"Her family was a subject she liked to avoid. Did her father desert the family, then?" Maybe it was a genetic thing.

"All I know is what Marianne told me when we were kids. According to her mother, she was conceived during a one-night stand on a holiday to Europe. She didn't even know the fellow's name."

How convenient, Gavin thought. It was hard not to feel bitter. When it came to Marianne, every path seemed to lead to a dead end. "What was her mother like?" he asked, fully prepared for Allison to avoid the question.

Surprisingly, she didn't.

"Adele was a teacher, like my father. She had Marianne when she was quite young, and she never married. She wasn't around their home much. She worked all day and 'socialized' most evenings. Marianne often had to fend for herself."

"Socialized?"

"That was the word Adele used. Not that she

fooled anyone. It was well known in town that Adele hung out with a younger crowd, drinking and, well, sleeping around."

He tried to muster some sympathy for Marianne. Could he blame her for not being a better mother, when she'd been raised so haphazardly herself?

Tory came running back. "Daddy, I'm thirsty."

He took her damp, slightly dirty hand in his. "Okay. Let's go back to the house. Allison, would you like to join us for an afternoon drink? I'd like to pay you a retainer and hear your other ideas about the house."

ALLISON HAD LOTS OF IDEAS about Gavin's house. She ended up staying for dinner so they could discuss them all. By the end of the evening, Gavin had written her a check and they had agreed to start work on Tory's room the following morning.

Allison knew of several good painters he could hire, but he wanted to do the painting himself. He didn't have many clients yet. Fixing up his home seemed like as good a way as any to keep busy.

"Let me help you," Allison offered. "I have no plans for tomorrow."

"Only if you accept payment at the standard rate." She tried to argue, but he stayed firm on that.

On Sunday morning at nine sharp Allison showed up in well-worn jeans, a white shirt knotted at the waist and her hair up in a ponytail.

He supposed it was a practical painting outfit and wasn't intended to look sexy. Following her up the stairs, though, it was impossible not to notice an inch of tanned skin through a tear just below the line of her right rear pocket.

From the landing, Allison peered into the open door of his office. Tory was on the floor, watching a movie on a portable DVD player. When she saw Allison, her face brightened. "Are you painting my room now? Can I help?"

"Later you can," Gavin promised. "But let us get started first, okay? When your movie is over, it'll be your turn to help."

It was the arrangement they'd agreed to this morning over breakfast and Tory seemed fine with it. He wasn't sure what he was doing and he wanted to figure things out for himself before he had to start supervising a six-year-old around paint.

"I prepped the walls last night," he told Allison

as they entered the bedroom. Tory's furniture had been pushed away from the walls and covered with old sheets. Until they were done in here, Tory would be sleeping in the guest room.

Allison ran her hand over the wall. "Nice and smooth. I can't even tell where the tape used to be."

"Is that what made all those marks?"

She nodded. "Marianne loved to cover her walls with pictures from art magazines."

He had that feeling of being dunked in cold water again. "This was her room?"

Allison's gaze was assessing. "You didn't know?"

"How could I?" Tory had chosen it for no apparent reason so far as he could tell. Aside from the master bedroom, all the rooms were about the same size and they all had dormer windows.

It was just chance that Tory had ended up in the same room as her mother.

Still, it was kind of eerie to think that Marianne had grown up in this very space. He wasn't a person to believe in signs, but there'd been a few. First finding this house, and now Tory picking Marianne's room.

But were they good signs or bad signs?

He supposed he'd find out once he saw Marianne again.

Allison spread a sheet of plastic on the floor, then used a Phillips screwdriver to pry the lid off a can of paint. When she was done, she handed him the screwdriver. "Want to take care of the electrical outlets?"

He looked at her, hoping she was going to explain exactly what she meant by that.

She raised her eyebrows. "You've painted before, right?"

"No. But how hard can it be?" He went to the light switch and then realized he was supposed to remove the plate. Sure. That made sense. He worked his way around the room, while Allison stuck green tape to all the baseboards.

Finally, it was time to actually apply the milky blue color to the walls.

Allison dumped some paint into one of the trays. "Would you rather roll or cut?"

He decided to play up his ignorance a little. "I thought we were going to paint."

She smiled, narrowing her eyes. "Maybe you should leave me in charge of the painting."

And miss out on the chance to spend a day

with her? "I admit I'm a novice. But I'm trainable."

"I hope so." Allison picked up a narrow paintbrush. "This is what we use for cutting. Basically you'll be painting around windows and baseboards. It requires a steady hand and precision."

He stepped close to her, put his hand on the brush. "I can be steady. I can be precise."

He was near enough to see her individual eyelashes as she dropped her gaze to where his hand was grazing hers. She let go of the brush, but he stayed where he was just a moment longer.

What was he doing—flirting with her? Well, so what if he was? Flirting was harmless enough. He didn't have to take it any further than that.

Anyway, she didn't seem to mind. She wasn't backing away. She was looking into his eyes, which was just what he was doing to her. And suddenly this didn't feel playful anymore.

"Allison?"

"Mmm?"

"Why did you and Tyler Jenkins break off your engagement?"

CHAPTER EIGHT

AT HIS QUESTION, Allison backed away. Gavin could tell she was uncomfortable.

"How do you know my ex-fiancé's name?"

"I saw his name on the wedding invitation I found lying on your porch. Also, he sent me an e-mail. Asked if we could get together to discuss a potential business opportunity."

"Wow, that was fast."

"How so?"

"I saw him yesterday on Main Street. He asked about you. Said he was looking for an architect to work on a big new construction project."

"That's what he told me, too. We're having lunch on Monday. He sounds like a straightforward kind of guy. Seems as if he's been successful, too."

She nodded.

"So what happened with the two of you?"

"It just wasn't right."

He wanted to know more. For some reason it was important to him. Probably because he was attracted to Allison and doing a damn poor job of fighting it.

If he was going to get involved with a woman again, he wanted to make sure he knew what he was getting into. "Any chance you'll get back together?"

"No."

"You sound pretty sure about that."

"I am."

Well, that part was good. He dipped his brush into the paint and started to work. Allison didn't say anything for the next five minutes, and Gavin started to worry that he'd offended her.

"I'm sorry for prying. I guess I shouldn't have done that."

"No problem. You've told me about your personal life. I shouldn't be surprised when you ask about mine. It's just that I've been fielding a lot of questions about the broken engagement lately. The subject's a little sensitive with me right now."

"It's never easy ending a serious relationship."

She sighed. "Not even when you're the one who wanted to end it, apparently."

He glanced over his shoulder at her. For some reason he'd assumed Jenkins had been the one to call things off.

"You look surprised. Trust me, you're not the only one. Everyone—including my father—is telling me I'm making a big mistake. But I had to go with my gut feeling on this one. The closer the wedding date came, the more anxious I felt. And you can't marry someone when you feel like that."

"No," he said, though he wasn't sure he agreed. Maybe Jenkins just hadn't been the right man for Allison. Or maybe Allison wasn't ready to make a commitment.

If the latter was true, then probably he'd be smart to keep his distance from her.

AFTER WORK on Monday night Allison helped Gavin paint the second coat in Tory's room, and on the night Allison had dinner with her father Gavin did the baseboards. He let Tory dabble with one of the brushes for short stretches of time, but generally he found it most productive to work after she was in bed. By Friday, he was able to put the electrical plates back on the wall and move the furniture into place.

"Daddy, am I supposed to sleep in my new room tonight?"

"Would you like to?"

She gave him an all-too-familiar shrug.

"You do like the room, right?"

"Yes."

He studied her face, not sure what he saw there. Though her opinion had been sought at every stage of the process, he'd noticed how closely Tory monitored Allison's voice and expressions, trying to gauge her opinions so she could mirror them.

Sometimes he wondered, did his daughter even know what she liked anymore?

"It's only a few more days until the drapes and the bedding are ready to be picked up." Allison was having them made professionally. "When they're done, you can move back into your room. Think you can wait that long?"

Tory hesitated, then nodded.

So he tucked her into the bed in the guest room again that night.

The next morning, after pancakes for breakfast and a drive downtown, Gavin and Tory found the perfect table to put in the dormer for her dollhouse. With the help of a sales clerk, Gavin loaded the table into the back of the station wagon. A few minutes later, as he wound his way back along Main Street, he found himself driving past The Perfect Thing. On impulse, he pulled into the first available parking space.

"This is Allison's store, isn't it? Are we going inside?"

Tory sounded excited. Exactly the way he felt, even though he shouldn't.

"Yeah, we're going inside. I need to find a painting for that blank wall in our entryway." Allison had been the one to suggest a painting for the empty space. She had several pieces at her store that might be suitable, she'd said.

He might as well check them out.

A breeze shot past as he held the door for Tory. A single golden leaf swept over his shoes, then settled against the brick foundation of Allison's store. He glanced up at a nearby birch tree. The colors were starting to change. In another week, summer would officially be over.

Inside the shop, Allison was talking to a customer, but she looked up at the sound of the door chime. Her neat features broke into a gentle smile, aimed at Tory, then sliding over to include Gavin.

Tory waved. "Hi, Allison."

Gavin put a hand on her head to stop her from running. "Allison's busy right now, squirt. She'll come and talk to you when she's free."

"Okay." Predictably, Tory headed right for the cabinet with the miniatures. Seeing that she was happy just to sit and look, Gavin worked his way around the store in a counterclockwise direction.

Various paintings were hung at intervals on the walls, and he stopped to study each of them. Two stood out from the rest, he decided.

One was a traditional landscape, with a genuine warmth that set it apart from the other paintings he'd seen. The second was more daring. Splashes of autumn colors suggested foliage. Dark trunks had been curved in such a way that they appeared to move.

He stepped close and admired the intricate brushwork. Then he stepped back and assessed the overall effect. He felt prickles at the back of his neck. Were they caused by the painting?

Or was it Allison, who was now standing just a few feet from his side?

"So what do you think?" she asked.

Gavin appeared to be focused totally on the painting. "Powerful."

She wondered what he would say if he knew he was looking at one of Marianne's works. At first, she considered telling him, but then she decided to let him judge the painting on its own merits. "I've always found this one provocative."

Actually, she found it disturbing, which was why she'd hung it in a corner where she rarely had to look at it. Since the day Marianne had brought it to her, almost a year ago now, she'd been hoping it would sell.

But not to Gavin.

"Who's the artist?" He stepped closer to the canvas so he could read the name painted in black on an angle in the lower right-hand corner. "Anna. No last name?"

Marianne had chosen that name to maintain her anonymity. Allison gave Gavin the same spiel she'd have given any other customer. "That's how she signs all her work. She's a New England artist with a unique impression-ist style."

"I feel like I've seen her work before, but I can't remember where. Would you recommend this piece?"

"As an investment? Definitely."

"Hmm. I'm kind of torn. It's fascinating. But

it also gives me an uneasy feeling. I'm not sure I could live with it on a day-to-day basis."

He'd described her own response to the painting perfectly.

"Is there anything else you like more?"

His gaze settled on her again, and something about the way he was looking at her made her feel as if he was saying that *she* was something he liked more.

After several long moments, he finally broke eye contact. "I like this painting by the window."

Gavin went to her favorite piece of art in the store. At first glance, it seemed to be just another pretty landscape.

"There's something about this one. I get a real sense of peace. And depth."

"Yes."

He met her gaze again. "You approve?"

"Yes."

Something warm pulsed between them. This man had a talent for challenging her emotions. She cleared her throat and reminded herself this was supposed to be a business transaction. "Would you like me to wrap it up for you?"

"Think it'll look good in the foyer?"

"I know it will."

"Then yes, please." He removed the large painting from the wall and carried it to the counter.

She measured a length of brown paper, folding the corners carefully. As she broke off a piece of tape, he held them down for her.

"I've got Tory's furniture back where it belongs," he told Allison. "And we just found a table for her dollhouse."

"Good. The drapes and duvet cover will be ready next week. I can bring them over Thursday night after work, if that would be convenient."

"That would be fine."

His voice was quiet, the tone deep and sexy. At least, she thought so. Her finger shook a little as she applied the final piece of tape.

She waited for him to leave, but instead he lingered. "Maybe you could stay for coffee on Thursday. I was hoping we could talk…"

Her heart thudded.

"About your plans for the rest of the house."

Of course, about the house. What had she expected?

"Sure, let's do that. Are you still planning to do most of the work yourself?"

"That depends. I had another meeting with your…with Tyler Jenkins. He's got big plans to build recreational properties near here and market them to urbanites in Concord and Rochester. Most would be condominiums and town houses, with some high-end cottages thrown in. If I got on board, it would mean regular working hours again."

"Is that what you envisaged when you moved to Squam Lake?" She remembered him talking about working from home and spending more time with Tory.

Gavin shrugged. "It's not unlike the job I had in Hartford. And a steady paycheck is always nice."

His answer disappointed her. She'd thought he would want to design one-of-a-kind cottages. Not cookie-cutter town houses and condos. But he did have a daughter to support. She shouldn't judge.

"Tory?" He picked up the wrapped painting. "Ready to go?"

She was cross-legged on the floor, next to the open cabinet. Allison had had no qualms unlocking it for her. Tory was admirably careful with the little figurines—which she clearly loved.

"Do we have to, already?"

That was the way Allison felt, watching them

leave. She was glad when new customers came in almost right away. She told herself she was *not* developing a crush on her new neighbor. She was not counting the days until Thursday.

AFTER WORK the next day, Allison stopped at the grocery store and then headed across town to her father's place. Her dad still lived in the house where she'd grown up, a modest bungalow on a heavily treed lot. She kicked her old tire swing as she walked past, sending it on a loopy trajectory, then hurried up the stairs, her feet crunching on a layer of brown leaves. The sugar maple in the front yard was always one of the first to lose its foliage in the autumn.

After shifting the groceries to free one of her hands, she opened the front door. "Dad?"

Nothing.

She walked inside and inhaled the indescribable yet familiar scent of home. She glanced past the old oak chair, piled high with her dad's sweaters. Several pairs of his shoes littered the hooked rug that her mother had made an eon ago.

Allison's mother had been gone for years, but her presence was everywhere. Allison couldn't walk into the kitchen without expecting to see her standing at the sink, her usual watchpost. She could swear that she even heard her mother's voice sometimes. *"Allison, is that you?"*

But of course there was no one in the kitchen as she set the groceries on the counter.

She wondered if her dad was as affected by her mother's absence as she was. Several times she'd suggested he move, but he always shook off the idea. "I've collected too much junk over the years. Besides, where would I go?"

She turned on the oven to preheat, then went out the side door to her father's workshop in the garage.

Since his retirement her dad had become serious about his wood carving, often working more than eight hours a day. Allison sold his pieces at her store. His loons were extremely popular and he was working on one of them now.

"Hey, Dad. That's looking good."

He pushed his glasses up onto his head, then surveyed the carving from several angles. "Is the neck too long?"

"It's beautiful. But it's time for a break. Come talk to me while I throw together a tuna casserole." She'd use her mother's recipe, which was one of her father's favorites. The man loved his comfort food.

He washed his hands before joining her, then opened the beer they always shared before dinner. "So, how's my beautiful daughter?"

She filled him in on recent happenings at the store and then on her design work. "I have a new client. It's the family that moved into the McLaughlin house."

"Oh?" He seemed vaguely interested at best. "What about your social life?"

"I haven't…"

"I saw Tyler this week. He asked about you."

"Speaking of Tyler. Did you ask him to fix the loose board on my porch steps?"

"I…"

"Dad, please. I know you mean well. But he's moved on and…"

"I only had to mention the loose board before he offered to fix it. Why would he do that if he didn't still have feelings for you?" He glanced at the empty chair to his right—the chair that had once been her mother's. "I want you to be happy. That's all."

This wasn't about her and Tyler at all, Allison realized. It was about her father and the fact that he still missed his ex-wife.

Why did she leave, Dad? The question was on

the tip of her tongue, just as it had been a hundred times before. But she couldn't make herself ask it. Instead, she spooned cheese sauce over the cooked pasta, flaked tuna and green peas, then put the casserole in the oven.

"Dinner will be ready in twenty minutes."

WHEN SHE'D FINISHED cleaning up after dinner, Allison played three rounds of cribbage with her father. She was home, as usual, by nine o'clock. Most of the lights were out already at the Grays' house. The night air was warm and she was tempted to check to see if Gavin was sitting out on the deck.

Two more days until Thursday...

Enough. Her father was right. It was time she put some effort into her social life. If she didn't have so much time on her hands, she wouldn't spend so many hours thinking about her appealing new neighbor.

As she fished her keys from her purse, she wished she'd left her porch light on. The nights were getting dark much earlier now.

She tensed as she heard footsteps on the gravel road behind her.

"Allison?"

His voice sent a shiver down her back. She swallowed, then turned around, knowing who she'd see and looking forward to the moment that she saw him smile. "Hi, Gavin."

He kept moving toward her, up the walk and onto the porch.

"Watch out for the loose board," she warned, just as he stepped around it.

"Were you at your father's?"

She nodded. He'd only lived in the house next door for about a month, yet already they were familiar with one another's routines. That wasn't so unusual. In Squam Lake neighbors looked out for one another.

"I don't suppose I could interest you in a glass of wine?" he asked.

Tory would be asleep at this hour. It would just be the two of them. "It's too late for wine, but maybe some tea?"

"I could do that." He held out his hand, and ended up touching her at the small of her back when she drew near. "Are you okay to sit outside?"

It was as if he'd read her mind as she was walking home. She nodded and let him guide her out to his deck. He had the heater glowing next to two cushioned chairs. Light jazz played softly from an outdoor speaker.

"Wow, this is nice."

"I managed to unpack a couple more boxes." He held out a chair for her to sit in. As soon as she was settled, he asked, "Is jasmine green tea okay?"

"Perfect." Allison let her head fall back and closed her eyes as Gavin went inside. Inhaling the musty smells of autumn and lake, she listened to the murmur of the wind in the trees. She felt entirely peaceful and yet, at the same time, anticipation tingled in her veins. She couldn't think of anywhere she would rather be right now.

"I love this time of day." Gavin was back. He handed her an oversized mug of tea with a warning that it was hot and sat in the chair next to hers, stretching out his legs.

"Are you a night person?"

"I didn't used to be. But when you have kids you grow to appreciate the quiet hour or two you have to yourself after they're in bed."

He spoke of kids in the plural sense. Allison hesitated, then asked, "Was Samantha a lot like Tory?"

"In looks, identical, but not in personality.

Sam was the adventurous one. She didn't learn to walk—I swear she started out running."

Allison chuckled. "She must have been a handful."

"You said it. When she was one she wiped out on the kitchen floor and whacked her head against the corner of the wall. Took four stitches that time. Then, at three, she was jumping on the bed and she fell and broke her arm. That was trip number two to the emergency room."

"What about Tory?"

"That one was born charmed. She never suffered so much as an ear infection. And I could always count on her to do as she was told. If I asked her to hold my hand when we walked along the sidewalk, she would hold my hand."

"Unlike her sister," Allison said softly, aware that they were venturing into darker territory.

Gavin set his mug on a nearby table. "Can I tell you about what happened? I'll understand if you don't want me to. It's… Well, obviously it's very upsetting."

Gavin was right—she didn't want to hear about Samantha's accident. But neither could she deny him the small comfort of sharing his pain. "I gather it happened on the way home from school?"

"We'd just left the classroom. We lived only four blocks away. I'd bought the house thinking it would be safer if the kids didn't have to take the bus."

He paused, letting the irony sink in.

"I can still feel Sam's hand in mine. Tory was on my right and Sam on my left, next to the curb. That proved to be our downfall. A woman was walking a dog on the opposite sidewalk. Sam loved dogs and she wanted to go pet this one. I tried to explain that we didn't have time. That the woman walking the dog was too far away and headed in the wrong direction."

Allison could picture it all vividly. Tory dutifully holding her father's hand. Her sister straining, calling out with excitement.

"It happened so fast. You don't know how many times I've played those moments over in my head. How could such a little girl slip out of my grasp so quickly? But she did. She darted between two parked cars and came out the other side at just the wrong moment."

"Oh, Gavin." His eyes were glazed. She hated to think of the scene he must be visualizing. It felt important to let him know he wasn't alone. She laid her hand on his shoulder.

"I was one second behind her. My fingers

grazed the edge of her raincoat, just as a motor-cycle flew through the school zone. Then came the most terrible sounds in the world. Sam's scream. The thud of the bike. The skid of the tires. The crash as it hit one of the parked cars."

Tory would have heard those sounds, too. How much had she seen? It would be a small mercy if those parked cars had obstructed her view.

"You aren't supposed to move an accident victim, but Sam was beyond saving. It was obvious. I cradled her in my arms and no one tried to stop me. Not the kid on the motorcycle, who somehow managed to emerge without so much as a scratch, and not the teachers who came rushing out of the school, either."

Allison imagined the chaos that must have erupted. Someone would have yelled, *"Call 911!"* People would have flooded out of the school and the nearby homes, then stood in clusters on the sidewalks, helpless.

"I'm not sure how much time passed, but the next thing I remember is that the woman who'd been walking the dog was holding Tory. I spoke to her later and she told me that Tory had stayed exactly where she was, as if she'd frozen there.

She said I yelled at Tory not to move when I ran after Samantha, but I don't have any memory of that."

"Oh, Gavin." There was nothing else to say.

"In some ways, Tory's been frozen ever since. In fact, she seems most like her old self when she's around you."

Allison recalled the way Tory rode her tricycle on moving day, like a small zombie. "She's bound to keep getting better, Gavin. She's young and resilient, right?" That was what people always said about children. "In addition to which, she has you."

Gavin turned toward her, his expression uncertain. "You think that's enough?"

"You're a terrific father."

"It's been a tough year. I haven't always been there for Tory. But it's getting easier. This move was a good idea. And I've started working again. This week I began plans for the sort of cottage I've always dreamed of designing."

"Is this for Tyler?"

"It's more customized than what he has in mind. This is something I'm working on just for fun—or until the right client comes along. I still haven't decided if I'm going to work with Jenkins Development or not."

"Oh?" She tried not to let her feelings about that show. It wouldn't be right to influence his decision.

"Tell me about Tyler. He used to be your fiancé. Obviously, you know him pretty well. Is he someone I would want to work with?"

She paused, choosing her words carefully. "Well, he's honest. And he's smart and hard-working. He built his company up from the small construction outfit his father had when he was a kid."

"Do I hear a 'but' in there?"

"Well, he is a little unimaginative, a little too rigid." And frankly, not that romantic, either. Though she doubted Gavin would care about the unromantic part.

"Yeah. I think I've already picked up on the rigid part. He has very definite ideas about this project, that's for sure." His look turned assessing. "But he must be an overall decent guy, if you were thinking of marrying him."

She nodded. If all Gavin wanted was a steady paycheck, he wouldn't go wrong working with Tyler.

And then Gavin shifted the conversation back toward the personal zone. "Do you miss him?"

She didn't have to think about her answer.

"No." She hesitated, then asked, "Do you miss Marianne?"

She'd surprised him with that one. He shook his head a little, as if clearing his mind.

"Marianne hasn't been part of my life for a long time."

And yet, he was still looking for her. Something about his explanation didn't add up. Warning bells should be ringing in her head, Allison knew, but with Gavin looking at her the way he was it was difficult to keep her distance.

She'd been feeling this shift in their relationship for a while now. A tension was building between them. The sort of tension that just begged for…

"Daddy," a plaintive voice called.

Allison started. She hadn't noticed the presence of a baby monitor until that moment.

Gavin's smile turned regretful. "Sorry, Allison. I need to check on her."

"Of course."

"Sometimes she needs me to lie down with her for a few minutes."

She understood what he was saying. "That's okay. I'll head home now and see you on Thursday."

This time it was he who put a hand on her shoulder. "I'll look forward to it."

Allison walked across the yard, through the damp evening grass. Once inside her own home, she checked the phone. There were no messages. She tidied a few things in the kitchen, then went back to the living room to look out the window that faced the Grays' house. All the lights were out. Good. Tory must have gone back to sleep easily.

And Gavin… Was he sleeping, too?

She was too wired to sleep herself, and now she wrapped her arms around her chest. There were still goose bumps on her skin, and they weren't from the cold. Something interesting was developing between her and Gavin. He'd given her several signals tonight. It would be hard to wait until Thursday to see him again.

She headed to the office to check her e-mail. There were several work-related messages that could wait for the morning, a couple of spam messages she was quick to delete and one personal message that stood out from the rest.

Every drop of warmth seeped from her body. She'd received an e-mail from Marianne.

CHAPTER NINE

ALLISON WAITED a moment before reading Marianne's e-mail. It seemed that her original message had gone through after all. And Marianne hadn't wasted any time replying. That wasn't usual for her. Something must be up.

Steeling herself, Allison scanned the message.

Hey, Allie, how are things in the old hometown? I hear via the grapevine that you canceled your wedding. You didn't even tell me you were engaged.

How could she have told her? Marianne hadn't been in touch since the last time she'd dropped off a batch of paintings.

And I hear a new family has moved into our old house. I'll bet you took them a casserole the very first night. What are they like? Good people?

Prickles danced on Allison's skin. Who had told Marianne all of this? As far as she knew, she was the only person in Squam Lake that Marianne bothered to stay in touch with.

More importantly…did Marianne know who her new neighbors were? She must. Marianne wasn't the type to show interest in anything that didn't concern her.

Allison was willing to bet that Marianne was being sneaky, trying to find out information without giving any herself.

As for me, I've parked my trailer in the White Mountains and I'm painting every day it doesn't rain. Could use some money. Maybe I'll bring some paintings around one of these days.

And that was it. The sum total of the message. Allison read it several times over and came to the unavoidable conclusion that Marianne was fishing for information about the new neighbors without admitting any prior knowledge of them herself.

Allison was sorely tempted to delete the message and pretend that she'd never received it. But she owed Marianne money for the last few paintings she'd sold. And if Marianne had more work to sell, she felt obliged to try and help.

Allison hit Reply. Good to hear from you, she typed automatically, even though it wasn't exactly true. She stared at the words on the screen a moment before deleting them.

That crack about the casserole. She knew when Marianne was being snide.

Glad to hear that you're doing well. Yes, I did cancel my engagement, and yes, I have new neighbors—a father and his young daughter. I think you may know them. Gavin and Tory Gray—sound familiar?

The questions sounded equally snide, even as she typed them. Allison backspaced as far as the word *daughter*. God, this was tough. She'd better just stick to business.

I've sold most of your paintings...just one left. The money is here waiting. Do you have Internet banking? I could transfer the funds that way.

Internet banking would eliminate the need for Marianne to come to Squam Lake.

Or I could mail you a check, if you have a postal address.

But Gavin wanted to see Marianne. He'd actually moved here thinking that meeting her mother might help Tory in some way. Despite her old ties with Marianne, Allison's sympathies were now fully aligned with Gavin and Tory.

A mother such as Marianne would not help Tory. But Gavin thought otherwise. Wasn't his opinion more important than hers, in this case?

It would probably be best if you came to Squam Lake, however. And I have room in my store to hang a couple new paintings, if you have them. I'll do my best to sell them for you.

She typed her name and hit Send before she could change her mind. Then she sat back in her chair and tried to figure out why she felt so terrible. The bad feeling churned inside her for several long minutes before she was able to label it.

Jealousy.

Gavin claimed to be searching for Marianne for his daughter's sake. But maybe he had unresolved feelings for her, too.

She didn't like thinking that Tory might actually belong to Marianne. And she really didn't like thinking that Gavin had once belonged to Marianne, as well.

And might again.

AFTER WORK on Thursday, Allison picked up the finished window treatments and bedding, then drove to Gavin's house. He and Tory were ready to help with the installation, dressed in jeans and old T-shirts.

Tory's room already looked great. Gavin had replaced her furniture. The dollhouse sat in the dormer on its new table and several framed pictures were hanging on the walls, including a collage of family photographs.

Allison's throat constricted at the sight of so many pictures of two young girls. All the pictures from now on would be of just one child.

"Here, Tory." Allison passed her one of the bags. Tory exclaimed over the pillows and duvet cover as she pulled them out.

But Allison's attention was still on the photographs. She'd spotted one of Marianne, holding two newborns in her arms.

There it was. The ultimate proof that Gavin's

story was true. Marianne was Tory's mother. Until she'd seen this picture, it hadn't felt quite so real to Allison.

Now the truth was indisputable. Studying the picture more closely, it seemed to Allison that Marianne's smile was hollow. Had she already known, when this picture was taken, that she would one day leave?

"You're going to have to explain how this works." Gavin was pulling the drapery hardware out of one of the bags, looking baffled.

"Of course." She dragged her attention back to the present and went over to help him. "There should be some printed directions in here, too." She dug into the bag and found them at the bottom.

As she handed the papers to Gavin, he said quietly, "Were you looking at the picture of Marianne?"

She nodded, and thought about mentioning the e-mail. Tory wasn't paying any attention to the two of them right now. She was busy trying to stuff her pillow into a ruffled sham and humming to herself.

But Allison didn't want the reality of Marianne to interfere with this moment. Who knew if the woman really was serious about coming to

Squam Lake, anyway? Why raise Gavin's hopes until Allison knew for sure?

She turned her attention to the drapery hardware. "This isn't as difficult as it looks." Holding up the pieces, she explained how they worked.

Gavin caught on quickly and while he screwed the hardware pieces into place, Allison helped Tory sort out the bedding. Half an hour later they were done. The curtains fit perfectly and the bed had been transformed into a cloud of pillows, eyelet and ruffles.

"We have one curtain left over," Gavin noticed.

"It's for the dormer. Sort of like a stage curtain." Allison held up the length of fabric to demonstrate. "Tory can close the curtain for a private playroom or open it like this." She pleated the soft cotton in her hands and tucked it back. "See?"

"Great idea." Gavin picked up the electric drill and Allison handed him one of the brackets. When they were done, she hung the curtain in place and then let Tory experiment, opening and closing it.

"Well?" she asked. Tory hadn't said one word about the transformation of her bedroom. "Do you like it? Are you happy with how your room looks?"

Tory's answer was in her big smile.

Gavin rested his hands on his hips and glanced

around with satisfaction. "This looks like a spread in *House Beautiful.*"

He was right. "Does it seem overdone? Too much white and lace?"

"Not at all," Gavin said. Tory's response was to dive on top of the bed and beam with pride.

Allison sighed with relief. "In that case, it's time for the final touch. This is for you, Tory." She pulled out one last item. It was a golden teddy bear in a Victorian gown and hat.

Tory gathered the bear into her arms and gave it a big hug.

"One room down," Gavin announced. "Eight to go."

Allison pretended to groan, then said, "If they're all as much fun to decorate as this one was, I'll be wishing your house was even bigger."

"Not me." Gavin gathered the tools he'd used and waited for Allison and Tory to leave the room before turning out the light.

He invited Allison to stay for supper, and afterward they sat out on the deck and watched as Tory blew soap bubbles out over the lake. When it was time to get ready for bed, Tory didn't argue.

"She's excited about her first night in her new

bedroom," Gavin commented as Tory ran off to change into her pajamas and brush her teeth.

"I'm glad she likes it."

"She loves it. And so do I. I'm anxious to see what you can do with the rest of the house."

"I noticed you've been patching the walls on the main floor. Want to start working here next?"

"Yeah. If possible, I'd like to have the living room and dining room ready for Tory's birthday. I was thinking of inviting my family from Hartford for the weekend."

Tory's birthday. That meant Sam's, too. "This will be the second birthday since the accident?"

"Yes." Gavin's jaw muscles tightened, then released. "As you can imagine, last year we didn't do much to celebrate."

She nodded, aching for him and Tory.

"But for Tory's sake, I want to make the day special. Plus, it'll be a chance for my mother and brothers to see the new place—if you think it can be presentable by then?"

"When's her birthday again?"

"The eighteenth."

"That gives us about three weeks."

"Pushing it, huh?"

"Yes…" She could see how much this meant to him, though. "But if we work weeknights and weekends, too, I think we could come close."

"That would be great." He gave her a considering look. "But it's not fair to ask you to give up so much of your time."

"Hey, I have no social life, remember?"

"I think that could be easily rectified."

Hot was the only way to describe the look that passed between them then. Allison felt an uneasy combination of nervousness and excitement.

"Is that an offer?" she asked.

Gavin put a hand on the small of her back. "It could be." He tilted his head, regarding her carefully. "But maybe you're not interested in a guy with a young daughter?"

She held his gaze as she said, "Tory is very lovable." *As is her father.*

Gavin pulled her closer. He was going to kiss her. It was just a matter of seconds. But then Tory came storming down the stairs.

"I'm ready for my bedtime story, Daddy."

They both laughed softly. Before dropping his hands, Gavin said, "Will you wait?"

"Yes."

ONCE TORY WAS ASLEEP, Gavin lit the gas heater and brought two mugs of tea out to the deck. He couldn't wait to be alone with Allison again and the feeling worried him.

She didn't seem to have any issues with children, which was good. And Tory liked her, which was good, as well.

But he wished he had a better understanding of why she'd broken off her relationship with Tyler Jenkins. Was it because she found him too rigid and unimaginative?

Or was it because she just wasn't ready to get serious about one man? It was important for him to know.

When he sat down again, they chatted about their jobs. He was just starting to feel comfortable when his phone rang.

Unhappy about the interruption, he checked the number before answering. He frowned when he saw the familiar office number. Hell, it was almost ten o'clock. Why was Matt still at the office?

"Allison, it's my older brother. I really should take this."

"I'll make some more tea." She gathered their mugs and slipped inside.

Glad that she hadn't decided to leave, Gavin hit the talk button. "Matt?"

"Hey, Gav. How are things?"

"I have a feeling they're a hell of a lot better here than there. Look out your window, brother. Can't you see that it's nighttime?"

"Yeah. Listen, Gavin, the reason I'm calling is to let you know that you shouldn't phone me at the house anymore."

"Huh?"

"Gillian asked me to move out. I've spent the past week sleeping on the sofa in my office."

Gavin had seen this coming. But the news still took his breath away for a second. "What the hell is going on there?"

"She saw me having lunch with a colleague last week—a female colleague. It was just a business lunch, nothing personal, but Gillian flew off her rocker and decided that was the last straw."

"Cripes. I can't believe this...." That wasn't quite true. He'd seen the cracks in his brother's marriage for a long time. Just last month he'd tried to make Matt promise to spend less time at work and more with his family. But now wasn't the time for recriminations.

"How are the kids?"

"Violet's fine, but Derrick's mad as hell."

"At his mother, for kicking you out?"

"Are you kidding? This is all my fault. Or so he thinks."

"What are you going to do?" Matthew couldn't live at the office indefinitely. Gavin paced the deck, feeling guilty because he wasn't in Hartford and couldn't offer his brother a spare bedroom.

Maybe he shouldn't have moved here, after all.

But he and Tory had needed this, needed to find a place where painful memories weren't waiting around every corner. And then there was Allison. He'd never have met her if he'd stayed in Hartford. "Can you bunk in with Nick?"

"Not an option. His place is tiny. Plus, you know what a slob he is. We'd end up killing each other before the first night was over. Don't worry. I've got a lead on a furnished apartment, just a few blocks from work."

Don't worry. Talk about impossible advice. "I don't suppose you could get a few days off and come out here?"

"You're all settled, then?"

"Well, not quite."

"That's what I thought. Anyway, I'm doing

okay—honestly. This break has been a long time coming."

True. But it still must hurt like hell. "All right, but I do want you to come for a visit. Think you could bring Mom and Nick out for Tory's birthday?'

"October eighteenth? I should be able to manage that."

"Good. And in the meantime, call me if I can do anything."

"Sure," Matt said, but even as they disconnected Gavin knew that he wouldn't phone. His big brother was used to shouldering his problems— and those of the rest of his family—on his own.

"I hope it wasn't bad news?" Allison returned, setting down the mugs of tea.

"My older brother and his wife have just separated." Gavin rubbed the back of his head, still a little bewildered by it all.

"I'm sorry. Maybe I should go?"

"No, I'd rather you stayed." He hadn't known Allison all that long. Maybe it was strange that he'd want her company at a time like this, but he did.

"Of course." She settled back in her chair.

"While I was waiting for the water to boil, I checked on Tory. She's sleeping soundly."

"That's great. She hasn't actually made it through the night entirely since Sam passed away. I'm hoping tonight might be the night."

"Nightmares?"

"No nightmares, fortunately. She just wakes up and wants to be reassured. The psychologist said it was pretty normal."

"I'm sure."

He took a sip of his tea, and stared out into the dark. "Matt and Gillian have been married thirteen years. Their son is twelve and their daughter is only five."

"This will be hard for them."

"Yeah. But it's not like they're used to having their father around that much. I'm afraid my brother is a workaholic. I've tried talking to him, but I don't think he could help it."

"Seeing how great you are with Tory, it's hard for me to imagine your brother not being the same. What was your dad like?"

"I can't remember much about him. He died when we were kids."

"I'm sorry."

"Well, we grew up fast after that. Mom was

used to Dad taking care of just about every-thing. We were lucky that he had insurance and a good pension. But Mom couldn't manage the money. Matt became the de facto head of the household."

"That must have been a lot of responsibility for a twelve-year-old."

"Exactly. I think my brother has forgotten how to have fun. Or even how to relax."

Allison tilted her head. The glow from the gas heater highlighted the angles of her cheekbones, the bronze highlights in her hair.

She was a pretty woman. Talented. Com-fortable to have around. Even when the going got tough. That was the real test, Gavin re-alized. Bad news had a way of sending most women running.

Apparently not Allison, however.

"How did your father's death affect you?"

"It wasn't as hard on me as it was on Matt."

She didn't look convinced, and he recalled something the grief counselor in Hartford had said to him. Something about him becoming his mother's emotional guardian and being drawn to needy women as a consequence. He wasn't sure what to make of that.

"And how about your mother? Is she doing okay now?"

"She was depressed for a long time. But when she turned seventy we found her a seniors' complex, and ever since she moved in there she's been better. They have an active social program. Scrabble every Wednesday, movie night on Friday, that sort of thing. Mom participates in everything. We have to book an appointment with her, if we want to visit."

Allison smiled and Gavin realized he didn't want to discuss his family anymore. Suddenly, all he could focus on was her eyes. And her lips. Her lush pink lips.

He sat forward in his chair, then leaned closer and took her hands. He rubbed at a paint stain on her fingernail, then studied her face again.

The look she gave him was open and trusting. In his heart, he knew that what was about to happen was something he didn't have the power to stop.

He leaned closer, angling his head until finally he felt her soft lips beneath his. She tilted her head, too, fitting her mouth perfectly to his.

Allison tasted as sweet as anything he'd ever experienced. He put his hand at the back of her neck. Curled his fingers through her hair. She returned his kiss on equal terms and he felt the flaring of desire.

Sometimes first kisses were awkward and uncomfortable.

Sometimes first kisses told you that you were with the wrong person.

But kissing Allison felt absolutely perfect. Which in its own way was the scariest thing of all.

CHAPTER TEN

THE NEXT MORNING Gavin's kiss was still on Allison's mind as she showed up for another day of painting. She was early, and Gavin and Tory were still in the kitchen in their pajamas.

"Sorry. I keep doing this to you, don't I?"

Gavin didn't kiss her hello, but he gave her a very warm smile. "As far as I'm concerned, you can keep on doing it. Sit down. I'll get you some coffee."

Tory was still in her chair, with an empty bowl in front of her, plus four different boxes of cereal and a carton of milk.

Gavin hadn't shaved yet, and it didn't look as if he'd combed his hair, either. He was wearing a gray T-shirt that clung to his broad shoulders and flat abs. His sweatpants seemed to hang from his hipbones.

"Coffee would be good." She forced her gaze from him to Tory. The little girl smiled.

"So what kind of cereal are you going to eat this morning?" Gavin asked his daughter.

Tory sighed, then turned to Allison, obviously hoping to be rescued.

"Hmm." Allison picked up each of the boxes and pretended to read the back of them while she was really studying Tory's face. "How about the oat flakes and crunchy nuts? Those look good."

Tory beamed at her.

"Okay, then." Since Gavin was busy with the coffee machine, Allison filled Tory's bowl, then added milk. As the child dug into her breakfast, Allison couldn't help but feel pleased. She seemed to be good at figuring out what Tory liked.

Allison asked how she'd slept in her new room. "Didn't wake up once all night." Gavin grinned, then set a mug in front of her. As she picked it up she noticed that it had left a wet ring on some blueprints he had on the table.

"Oops."

"No worries. Those are just rough sketches. I'd like to run up and change. Will you two be okay for five minutes?"

"Sure." She picked up one of the drawings. It

was a rendering of the exterior front of a cottage, with river-rock columns and a generous porch.

She liked it very much.

Allison took a sip of her coffee. The hit of caffeine was just what she needed to counter the effect of seeing Gavin in the clothes he'd been sleeping in.

A coloring book and crayons were on the table next to Tory's cereal bowl and when she was finished eating she went back to work on a picture she'd started earlier.

Allison complimented her on the good job she was doing and Tory asked her to pick a color for the doghouse in the picture.

"Red?"

"Yes!" Tory chose that crayon from the box and started filling in the space intently, her tongue peeking out from the corner of her mouth.

Allison picked up a pencil Gavin had left next to his drawings. She added foundation plantings, some outdoor furniture for the porch, a tree out front and an old-fashioned rustic mailbox.

At the sound of his footsteps, she stopped her doodling.

"Okay," he said. "I'm ready to get to work."

"Great." Allison stacked his papers out of the way. "First, we need paint."

"Sounds like a trip to the hardware store is in order."

"We haven't chosen colors yet," she reminded him. "I brought my color wheel with me. Hang on. I'll get it."

As she left her chair, Gavin started clearing the table. She saw him pick up the drawing she'd been doodling on for a closer look.

"You said it wasn't important?" When he didn't answer she added, "I didn't ruin anything, did I?"

GAVIN ADMIRED THE ADDITIONS Allison had made to his rendering. He'd designed a house. And in ten minutes, with a few simple strokes of a pencil, Allison had taken that house and turned it into a home. What she'd added looked so appealing that he wanted to open the front door, go inside and never come out again.

"Gavin? I'm sorry. I thought they were just rough sketches…."

"They are. Please don't worry. I like it. Have you ever worked with an architect before?"

"Only on renovations. A brand-new house would be fun."

He knew they'd work well together. They'd proven that already with his own house. "I had a call the other day from some prospective clients. If I get the job, I'll introduce you to them."

Her eyes lit up. He knew she liked the idea.

For a moment he had the sensation of being over his head again. Only, this time the water was warm and enticing. It was a little scary how well suited he and Allison seemed to be, on every level from professional to personal.

But it was exciting, too.

He felt a tug on his arm. "Daddy?"

Embarrassed by the realization that he'd been staring at Allison when his daughter was present, he gave his head a mental shake. "Yes, Tory?"

"What color do you like?" Tory showed him Allison's color wheel.

"I've narrowed the choices to a few options," Allison explained. "Let's take them to the living room and see which you and Tory prefer."

They sat on the sofa, and Gavin ended up next to Allison. Her hair had a fresh shampoo smell. Then there was that worn spot on her jeans. Everything about her made him want to touch her.

"So." He cleared his throat. "What are your ideas about colors?"

"I was thinking we'd paint the main rooms in rich tones, then use a neutral palette for the hallways and foyers."

She spread the color options over her lap and proceeded to talk about the pros and cons of various combinations. Eventually, Tory grew bored and wandered upstairs.

He and Allison were alone.

"What do you think of this? Amber for the living room and dining room, forest green for the kitchen and sandy taupe for the hall and foyer?"

"Is that what you'd pick?"

"Gavin." He heard amusement in her tone. "You're starting to sound like Tory."

"That's because I can't think when you're this close to me."

Her eyes widened.

"Your jeans are very distracting, Allison." He reached out and stroked a tiny bit of exposed skin on her knee. "Especially what's under them."

"What are you doing?"

She didn't try to stop him, he noticed. He put a hand to her hair. It was every bit as smooth and soft as it looked.

"I couldn't sleep at all last night because I was thinking of you."

Her green eyes seemed to glow. "I couldn't sleep, either."

"I can't be around you every day and not want to touch you."

She said nothing to that, but she wasn't pulling away. From what he could tell, the attraction between the two of them was mutual.

He took her hands and the color wheel slipped to the floor. "You know what I was thinking when I couldn't sleep last night?"

"I'm almost afraid to ask."

"Don't worry. It wasn't X-rated. At least, not all of it. I was thinking that you were too good to be true. Are you sure you don't have any skeletons in your closet?"

She hesitated. "Depends what you mean by skeletons, but I don't think I do."

"Lucky me, then," he murmured. He leaned in for the kiss he'd been craving all morning.

"Yes," she whispered, leaning forward, too.

Before he could meet her in the middle, the sound of Tory stomping down the stairs cut him short. "I found my books, Daddy." Tory raced into the room, fortunately oblivious to the fact that they were holding hands. "Did you guys pick out colors yet?"

WHILE THE OWNER of the hardware store mixed their paint, Allison wandered up and down the aisles with Gavin and Tory trailing behind. She noticed a light fixture that would work in the main bathroom. "What do you think of this, Gavin?"

"I like it."

She jotted down the cost and product number in her notebook.

It was fun shopping with Gavin and his daughter. Just as it had been fun to drive downtown with them in the red station wagon. She felt a bit like she was playing at the role of wife and mother, and the fit was not that bad. Not bad at all.

"Dad, can I look at the toy section?"

"Sure, squirt. I'll come with you." He gave Allison a warm smile. "Give me a holler if you come up with any other ways to spend my money, okay?"

"You can count on that." Warmth spread through her as she turned up the next aisle. Here were faucets and sinks, and she made note of several that would work with her plans.

Ever since Gavin had almost kissed her in the living room this morning, her mood had been spiraling upward. Maybe it was too soon after her breakup with Tyler, but meeting the right guy wasn't something you could schedule. She was free. Gavin was free. Why shouldn't they—

She rounded a corner and almost walked into her father. "Hi, Dad. What are you doing here?"

"My reading lamp burned out last night." Her father peered at the array of lightbulbs on the shelves in front of him. "Can you tell which of these bulbs is right for a tri-light? I should have brought my damn glasses with me."

Allison scanned the selection, then pulled out the box he wanted.

"Thanks, Allie." He squinted at her. "What are you up to today? You look good. Happy." He snapped his fingers. "Let me guess. You and Tyler…"

"There's been no change with me and Tyler. I'm here with my new client. Buying paint."

"Oh?"

"It's the new neighbor I was telling you about, Dad." Just on cue, Gavin appeared, obviously looking for her.

"Well, how much poorer am I now?" he asked, coming up behind her, touching her elbow.

"Gavin Gray, this is my father, Seth Bennett. Dad, this is my new neighbor."

The men took stock of one another and Allison could tell her father was impressed. When Gavin turned away for a second to call for his daughter, her dad gave her a wink and a nod of approval.

She felt a little embarrassed. Her dad really was the most incorrigible matchmaker, and she was almost certain Gavin had seen the wink, too. But at least her father wouldn't keep harping about Tyler now.

Then Tory came running toward them and everything changed. At the first sight of the child, her dad turned pale.

She heard him swear under his breath, and her father never swore.

"Dad, this is Gavin's daughter, Tory. She's just started grade one this year."

"Good God. What's going on here?" Her father poked his index finger at Gavin's chest. "Who are you, really?"

"Dad." Allison was mortified. She'd told her father that the new neighbor had a child. Unless it was the resemblance to Marianne that had him spooked?

She grabbed his arm and led him away, before

he had a chance to upset Tory further. "What's the matter with you?"

"That girl. She's looks just like…"

"I know. She looks like Marianne McLaughlin. That's because Marianne was her mother."

Her dad's face grew really pale then. "Is that true? But Marianne isn't married."

"She and Gavin never made their relationship legal. But Tory is their daughter." She considered explaining about Samantha, but this wasn't the time for that. "Marianne deserted them, Dad. Gavin and Tory have moved to Squam Lake hoping for a fresh start."

Her father simply stared at her. It was a lot to take in, she had to admit.

"That girl is Marianne's daughter?"

"Yes. But the only parent she really knows is Gavin. Marianne deserted her when she was only one year old." She emphasized the age, wanting her father finally to understand the sort of person Marianne really was.

Her dad ran a hand over his face, as if he wanted to block out the truth of what she was saying. "Poor Marianne," he said softly.

"Don't you mean *poor Tory?*"

But he didn't answer her. Frown lines settled

heavily on his face, as he thought about all she'd told him. "This Gavin Gray fellow. He's more to you than just your neighbor and client, isn't he?"

"No." Not yet, anyway.

"You can't kid a kidder. I know what I saw when the two of you looked at each other."

"Well, maybe. But why not? You seemed really anxious for me to find someone new the other day at dinner."

"Not this guy."

"I thought he made a good first impression." Until his daughter appeared on the scene.

"This man isn't looking for a fresh start in Squam Lake."

"Why do you say that?"

"He's looking for Marianne."

"Well, yes. But that's for Tory…"

"Bull." Her father swore again. "Things may be all lovey-dovey now, but I suggest you think about what's going to happen when he finds Marianne."

She thought about the dratted e-mail and wished she'd just deleted it. "I imagine they'll talk about their daughter. Gavin wants her mother to be part of Tory's life."

"Maybe he wants more than that. Stay out of this, Allison. You don't want to be the woman who comes between and a man and the mother of his child."

CHAPTER ELEVEN

ALLISON DID HER BEST to ignore her dad's words. He didn't know what he was talking about. Gavin and Marianne had never been married. They hadn't seen one another in six years. She had no reason to feel guilty about starting a relationship with Tory's father.

She and Gavin spent the afternoon painting, stopping only to have a pizza for dinner and to go out for an evening stroll with Tory riding her tricycle between them. Once the little girl was in bed, they finished the living room and carried on down the hallway until, at ten, they collapsed wearily on the couch.

"Maybe we should be pacing ourselves." Allison's neck and shoulders were aching. She could only guess that Gavin felt just as sore, since he'd been doing the ceiling.

"Sit and rest," he told her, and she obligingly

flopped onto the sofa, closing her eyes and letting her legs sprawl out in front of her.

She felt the cushions sink as Gavin settled beside her. Next, she felt his touch on her leg.

"You have a new tear in your jeans."

His fingers were taking her mind completely off the aches and pains in the rest of her body. She opened her eyes. "Doesn't matter. I was going to throw them out anyway."

"Don't you dare."

Adrenaline and desire buzzed inside her at the implication. He slid a finger between the frayed threads and explored the soft skin above her knee.

Allison shifted to face him.

They stared at each other a long time.

"I see two options here," he said finally.

She raised her eyebrows.

"This might be a good time to ask what was up with your father this morning."

She acknowledged this with a slight movement of her head. "Or?" she prodded.

"Or I could kiss you."

Her answer was in her eyes, even before she shifted forward on the couch. He slid an arm around her back, pulling her closer. Their lips were only inches apart.

"I have a feeling your father wouldn't approve of what's about to happen here."

"I thought we'd just decided on option two, not option one."

"You're close to your father. I'd rather have his approval."

"I just had my thirtieth birthday. I think I'm beyond needing my father's okay before I kiss someone."

"Thank God for that."

She laughed softly. "Enough conversation."

Finally, he pulled her a final two inches closer. Their lips met, tenderly at first, then more passionately. She loved the way Gavin kissed her, as if she were someone special, to be savored. But after a few moments, she could tell he wasn't fully into the moment. Not the way he'd been the first time.

"What's wrong?"

"I just can't stop wondering, why did your father react the way he did?"

"He…" She ran her tongue over her lips, even though they were already moist. "Dad was really attached to Tyler. He wants me to patch things up with him. Maybe he saw you as a threat to his hope that that might happen."

"But it wasn't until he saw Tory that he seemed disapproving."

She could tell this had hurt Gavin. "It wasn't seeing Tory that upset him. It was the resemblance to Marianne."

"He spotted it that quickly?"

"I guess so." She sighed. "There's something I've been meaning to tell you."

He drew away, his expression cautious.

"It's Marianne," she said finally. "I sent her an e-mail and yesterday I heard back from her."

Gavin tensed. "What did she say?"

"She's thinking of coming to town."

"When?"

"I'm not sure. Marianne isn't big on planning."

"Right." He ran his fingers through his hair. She could tell she'd unbalanced him with the news.

"I wonder how you'll feel about her when you see her again."

He studied her eyes. "It won't change anything between you and me, if that's what you're wondering."

That was what she'd wanted to hear. And yet she didn't feel reassured. Gavin could guess at his reaction, but he wouldn't really know how he felt about Marianne until he saw her again. He'd already admitted to being fascinated by her at the beginning. There was no guarantee he wouldn't fall under her spell again.

THE NEXT MORNING Gavin awoke to the sound of the phone ringing. He was surprised to see that it was past nine in the morning. Call display showed the name Matthew Gray. Not the office number, but one he didn't recognize. With a premonition of bad news, he pressed the talk button.

"Matt? Where the hell are you?"

"I moved into that furnished apartment I told you about."

At the hollow sound of his brother's voice, Gavin knew he was feeling low. "You okay?"

"This is my first weekend away from my kids. I'm staring at a tacky print hanging over the sofa and wondering what in the hell I'm doing here."

Maybe you should go to the office, Gavin almost said. But being a workaholic was what had landed Matt in this mess in the first place. "Invite the kids over," he suggested instead.

"Gillian set up a schedule. I get them next weekend."

"That sucks." Gavin couldn't imagine only seeing Tory according to some schedule.

"Big-time," Matthew agreed.

"Well, go for a workout. Or visit Mom. See how she's doing."

"Believe it or not, I've done both those things already. I was up at six, at the gym half an hour later. Then I showered and took Mom out for breakfast. She's doing great, by the way. Was in a big rush to get back for lawn bowling. Couldn't get out of my car fast enough."

"At least she's happy."

"Not about the breakup, she isn't. She gave me a blast over breakfast. Not that she ever seemed to like Gillian that much."

"She's worried about the kids," Gavin guessed.

"So am I. I'm afraid that when next weekend rolls around, they won't even want to visit. It's pretty drab here, bro."

"Go out and invest in some computer games. Or maybe get an Xbox or something."

"They have one at home. They have *all* the latest gadgets. I guess Gillian and I spoiled them."

"Pick up tickets to a ball game, then. That would be even better."

"Yeah, maybe I'll do that."

But Matt sounded so dispirited, Gavin doubted he would. Maybe Nick could get the tickets. When the call was over, Gavin dialed his younger brother's number. As the phone rang, he crossed the hall to check on Tory.

She wasn't in her room. Her bed was made. She must be downstairs.

The phone was still ringing as he made his way down the stairs. His brother's shifts were always changing, so it was impossible to figure out his schedule. He'd probably have to leave a message on the machine.

He found Tory at the kitchen table, eating a bowl of the same cereal she'd had the day before.

"Hey, squirt." He patted the top of her head, then went to the cupboard to get his own bowl.

"Hi, Daddy," she said just as Nick answered on the other end of the line.

"Huh?"

"Nick?"

"Is this Gavin?" Nick didn't sound pleased.

"I woke you?"

"Hell yes, you woke me. It's nine o'clock on a Sunday morning. Some of us have social lives, you know." In a softer, sweeter tone, he said, "Sorry, Linda. I'll take this in another room."

There was a pause, while Nick got out of bed and left the bedroom. Gavin filled his bowl with cereal, then added milk.

"Okay." Nick's tone was brisk now, full of business. "So what's up?"

"What happened to Emily?"

He waited through Nick's answer, without paying much attention. The next time he called it would be someone new, anyway. Nick was getting too old for this. But Gavin had bigger problems today.

"Have you talked to Matt lately?" he asked.

"I heard he was moving into an apartment."

Gavin gave him the latest, including Matt's new phone number. After Nick had promised to look into ball tickets for the following weekend, he asked him about Tory's birthday.

"Think you'll be able to come? Maybe give Mom a lift, too?"

"I'm on nights that week, but I'll work a switch to make it happen," Nick promised.

"Thanks." Gavin knew it was a promise he could count on. Nick wasn't big on commitments, but when he made them, they stuck.

With that phone call finished, Gavin kissed his daughter's cheek. "That's from Uncle Nick."

Tory smiled, then glanced out the kitchen window. "Is Allison coming over today?"

"Yes. It's going to be another day of painting. Think you can handle it?"

"I like it when Allison comes over."

"Yeah, I noticed." And so did he. As far as he was concerned, they were going to be finished painting this house far too soon.

ALLISON SPENT all her spare time the following week at Gavin's place. On the weekend, they went to Concord to shop for furniture, rugs and art. They filled the back of the station wagon with purchases that would help transform 11 Robin Crescent into a real home.

On the drive back to Squam Lake, they stopped for a late lunch at a diner at the side of the highway. The woman who showed them to their booth, then brought glasses of ice water, was clearly the wife of the cook.

"Tell them the specials, Gloria," he hollered from the kitchen.

She rolled her eyes. "As if I'd forget."

When Gloria left them to mull over their choices, Gavin leaned back with obvious satisfaction. "I'll take a family-owned business over a chain restaurant any day."

"I agree." Their tastes were similar in so many ways. Maybe it was a sign. Or maybe she just wanted it to be. Allison opened the plastic-coated menu and smiled.

"See something you like?" Gavin asked.

She let her gaze linger on him for a moment. "Yes."

"What do you think I would like?" Tory asked, sounding concerned.

"Hmm." Allison surveyed the kid selections. "Chicken fingers and fries?"

Tory smiled, then nodded. "I need to go to the bathroom."

"It's right there." Gavin pointed at a door between the eating area and the kitchen. Watching his daughter leave the table, Allison felt a buzz of anticipation. Much as she enjoyed Tory, she'd come to treasure the few stolen moments she and Gavin had together.

Expecting him to sneak a kiss or at least reach across the table for her hand, she was surprised to see a worried expression settle on his face.

"Is something wrong?"

"Probably not. But I've noticed Tory expects you to make a lot of her decisions for her."

Was he bothered that his daughter didn't rely on him as much as before? "Is that a problem?"

"Maybe not. But when Tory and I met with the new therapist we talked a little about you."

"Oh?" She knew they'd gone to North Conway for an appointment on Wednesday, but she hadn't heard anything else about it.

"Most of the talk was positive. Tory likes you very much and that's a good thing. But the therapist did say that we have to be careful Tory doesn't make you a sort of 'twin substitute' for Samantha. In other words, we need to help Tory learn to make her own decisions."

"Oh." Allison tried not to feel hurt. Here she'd been thinking it was great that she and Tory had this connection, and actually it wasn't.

"I'm not suggesting anything drastic. I don't want to upset Tory. But if you could gently encourage her to make up her own mind now and then, that would be best."

"Of course." She forced herself to smile. Gavin hadn't meant to come across as critical. At least she didn't think he had. But his talk made her wonder exactly what was going on with the two of them.

They were more than just client and consultant to one another. Tory was with them most of the time, but there'd been a few more late-night kisses this week, each one sweeter and more intense than the one before.

Up until this moment she'd been sure that Gavin was into her as much as she was into him. The fact that he hadn't actually asked her out was because there'd been no time.

It had nothing to do with Marianne's pending visit.

Later, when they weren't so busy, there'd be opportunities for dates.

THE NEXT SUNDAY Allison was up late helping Gavin shift his plates and glasses into the newly painted cupboards. She'd had them professionally finished in a beautiful cream, with an antique wash.

As a result, she was late opening the shop on Monday morning. She unlocked the back door at ten-thirty, dumped her bag behind the counter, then flipped over the Open sign to face the street. She hadn't even had time to check the messages or open the register when the door chimes sounded.

She looked up to greet her first customer with a smile. Only to freeze at the sight of Marianne standing in the doorway, a large canvas in her arms.

"Any chance you could help me with this?"

For a second Allison couldn't speak. Marianne had clearly taken no pains with her appearance. Her jeans hung loosely on her too-skinny frame and her T-shirt was splattered with paint. Her hair was wild and her face bore no visible traces of makeup.

Yet she was more beautiful than ever. Her skin was paler, flawless, accenting the deep blue of her eyes and the darkness of her hair.

It wasn't fair. Normal women couldn't compete with Marianne.

"Allison?"

"Sorry." She hurried around the counter and took one end of the painting. "Let's take this to the back until I can figure out where to hang it. So…when did you get into town?"

And when are you planning to leave? she wanted to add.

"Late last night." She paused, then added, "I drove by my old house."

"Oh."

"You told me a father and his daughter were living there, right? But I saw a woman through the kitchen window. I could have sworn it was you."

CHAPTER TWELVE

ALLISON HAD NOTHING TO HIDE and no reason to feel guilty. "Yes, that was me." She sounded calm and reasonable. Or so she hoped.

"Oh?"

Allison suppressed the urge to explain why she had been at Gavin's house so late. It really wasn't any of Marianne's business.

"Put the painting down here," she said. They propped the canvas against the far wall and Allison stood back to admire it. The piece was abstract, disturbing, powerful. Right away she could tell that this was superior to anything Marianne had painted before. "You keep getting better."

"You think?" Marianne gave the canvas an offhand glance. "It's difficult for me to be objective."

"This belongs in a real art gallery." Her customers were looking for comfortable pieces that would add beauty to their homes. Marianne's work, as good as it was, was too challenging to sell well at The Perfect Thing.

"I've got at least twenty more paintings done."

"That many?"

"I need to sell them, Allie. I need the cash."

The careless manner was gone now. Marianne sounded almost desperate. Whatever her other flaws, Marianne had never been materialistic. "I've got your check here." Allison opened the cash register and pulled it out.

Marianne accepted the payment eagerly. "Thanks." She glanced at the amount. "You didn't keep a commission?"

Allison shrugged. "It sounded as if you were pretty strapped."

"I am."

Allison waited, but no details were forthcoming. She couldn't be surprised about that. If Marianne hadn't told her about Gavin and the twins, she was probably keeping other secrets, as well.

"Look, Marianne, I'll try to sell this piece, but I have to be honest. Your more recent work doesn't appeal to my customers the way the earlier paintings did.

"I know a few art dealers in Concord. If you're really serious about selling your work, why don't you see if any of them would be interested in representing you?"

"I've already started making a few inquiries," she admitted. "But if you have some contacts, I'd be glad to talk to them."

"Hang on." Allison went to the computer and sorted through her address book. While she compiled a list, Marianne strolled through the shop.

"The place looks even better than when your grandma was running the business."

"Thanks." Allison hit the print button, then handed Marianne a list of dealers. "Good luck. Let me know if you have any success."

"I will."

Marianne was poised to leave, and frankly that was what Allison would have preferred. But some impulse made her say, "So…do you have time for coffee?"

She could tell Marianne hadn't expected the invitation, but she shrugged. "Why not?"

Allison led the way to the small kitchen area. "How long are you here for?" Except for when her mother died, Marianne's visits to Squam Lake had never lasted more than twenty-four hours.

"I'm actually staying awhile."

Just her luck Marianne would pick this time for an extended visit. "Where?"

"At a friend's."

"Oh?" As far as Allison knew, she was the only "friend" Marianne still had in Squam Lake. But Marianne offered no further explanation.

"Want a latte or a cappuccino?"

"Black coffee suits me fine." Marianne slid into a chair, resting her elbows on the table. "So what's new with you? I heard you came this close to marrying Tyler Jenkins." She held up her thumb and forefinger so they were practically touching.

"That's true, but I got cold feet. He's dating someone else already, so I guess I wasn't hard to replace." She pushed a button for regular coffee, then set a mug under the spout. "How about you? Any man in your life?"

"Not at the moment. But tell me about your neighbor. I hear he has a daughter. Is that right? Just one?"

As Gavin had suspected, she didn't know about Samantha. Allison took a deep breath. She had to proceed with caution here. She waited as the dark roast finished dripping into the mug. When it was done, she turned to Marianne.

"Let's stop pretending, okay? I know about you and Gavin. And about the twins."

Marianne blinked.

"I realize we haven't been close since you moved away. But you might have mentioned that you were pregnant, Marianne. That's kind of a big omission."

"It wasn't something I wanted to talk about."

"Obviously."

"Don't look at me that way. I didn't want kids. I told Gavin I didn't want them, but he made me go through with it. And I tried, Allie. Really I did." Marianne brought the coffee mug to her lips with trembling hands. She took a sip. Composed herself.

"I can't describe the way I felt at that time. Depression doesn't scratch the surface. I was stifled. Drowning. There was no time for me to take a shower, let alone spend time on my art. Believe me, leaving the twins was as much for their safety as it was for my sanity."

"You could have visited them. You didn't even leave a forwarding address."

"Yeah. You make it sound so easy. But I was beyond rational by then. Mom dying was the last straw. I had to split."

Allison thought about Marianne's art. Was this where those disturbing elements had come from—the pain of abandoning children she hadn't wanted in the first place? "Where did Gavin factor into the equation?"

"He was just a guy. Our relationship wouldn't have lasted another month if I hadn't become pregnant."

How could she talk about him like that? "Gavin is a good person, and he's a terrific father. Very giving and compassionate."

"Yeah, I know. But I was young. And I wasn't interested in spending my life with a saint. I could never live up to that standard." Marianne tilted her head and her exquisite blue eyes narrowed. "Are you going to tell me why you were at his house last night? You two sleeping together?"

"Marianne!"

"Well, you're both single consenting adults. It wouldn't be a crime."

"He's my client, okay? We were painting."

"At ten o'clock on a Sunday night?"

"His family is planning a visit soon. He wants the house ready for them." Allison stopped before mentioning the birthday party. But Marianne made the connection anyway.

"They must be coming for the girls' birthday."

Girls. Whoever was feeding Marianne her information didn't know about Samantha's accident. "You should talk to Gavin about this."

"You think he'd speak with me?"

"Why do you suppose he moved here?"

A light gleamed in Marianne's eyes, making Allison uneasy.

"He moved to my hometown. He *wants* to see me."

The uneasy feeling grew. "Yes, he does."

"I suppose he's at work right now."

Allison hesitated. She wasn't keen on facilitating this meeting. But it was what Gavin had wanted for so long. She had to let it happen. "Gavin works from home."

"Oh." Marianne finished her coffee, then stood up. "See ya later, Allie. Thanks for the check."

Allison had to ask. "Are you going to Gavin's now?"

"Maybe. It might be interesting to see the old place."

The old place. Was that really all she was interested in? What about the guy who'd fathered her babies? And what about the children themselves? Tory and Samantha seemed to be the last items on Marianne's list of priorities. Was she even going to care when she heard what had happened to Samantha?

THE REST OF THE DAY was torture for Allison. She wanted to know how things were going with Gavin. How had he reacted when Marianne showed up at his door—had he invited her in? How long had they talked? Maybe they were still talking now.

At noon, Gertie Atwater arrived for her afternoon shift. She noticed Marianne's new canvas right away.

"Don't tell me that woman is back in town." She stepped around the painting as if she suspected it might be contaminated with the Ebola virus.

"We need to find a place to hang that."

"It will never sell."

"Probably not. But Marianne's a friend."

Gertie sniffed. "That depends on your point of view. I know your mother would have agreed with me on this—she never brought anything good into your life. The sooner she leaves town, the better."

At three-thirty Allison thought about Tory. Would Gavin and Marianne pick up the little girl from school together? It was difficult to imagine.

The entire situation was difficult to imagine. Gavin was certain Marianne would have a healing effect on Tory, but Allison wasn't convinced. The Marianne who had stood in her shop this morning had shown not the slightest degree of maternal instinct.

But maybe, as her father had hinted, Gavin's real motivation for finding Marianne had nothing to do with Tory.

Marianne had been beautiful when he'd met her all those years ago. She was even more stunning now.

If Gavin hadn't gotten over her, Allison wouldn't be surprised.

Finally, Allison could stand the waiting and wondering no longer. "I'd like to leave a little early today. Would you mind if I left you alone for a few hours?"

"No problem," Gertie said without hesitation, even though the day had been busy and there were several customers milling around the floor as they spoke. "Are you feeling okay, dear?"

"I'm fine. I just need to check on a client."

"If you say so. But if you need to talk…"

"Gertie." Allison gave her a hug. She guessed her most faithful employee was thinking of Tyler, the breakup and the canceled wedding. "Are you and my father in cahoots? At least once a day he tries to talk me into patching things up with Tyler."

Gertie laughed at the idea. "Men are such fools. I never thought Tyler was the right man for you."

"Really?"

"Now, Gavin Gray on the other hand…"

ALLISON HURRIED along the sidewalk, her stomach tightening with nerves as the old McLaughlin house came into view. How had the mother-daughter reunion gone?

Allison tried to keep her focus on Tory rather than on Gavin. But it was impossible not to wonder how Marianne's reappearance was going to affect their relationship. Not that long ago she and Gavin had been just clients and neighbors. Now they were on the cusp of becoming something more.

Not until Marianne had shown up at the store had Allison realized just how much she wanted their relationship to continue. And how afraid she was that Marianne had the power to stop that from happening.

Gertie was right. Her mother had never liked Marianne. Abigail Bennett hadn't said much when Allison was around, but sometimes after she went to bed Allison had heard her parents arguing.

Always, it was the same thing, with her mother listing all Marianne's faults, and her father sticking up for her. Marianne's mother worked at the same school he did, and he felt sorry for both of them. "It isn't easy being a single parent. Or being a kid without a father."

That was his standard excuse whenever Marianne did something that Allison's mother deemed unacceptable. For example, the time she stole Allison's date a week before prom.

Allison stopped in front of Gavin's house, wishing she had an excuse to knock on the door. She'd been hoping to find them outside, but though the weather was fine and the red station wagon was parked in the drive there were no signs of life.

Maybe she could pretend to want his opinion in regard to a swatch of fabric or a piece of furniture that she'd found for his house. But subterfuge was something she'd never mastered.

She'd just have to go home and wait.

And then his front door opened. "Allison?"

Gavin stepped out and she felt an unmistakable longing, simply at the sight of him. How could Marianne ever have left a man like him?

"Hey, there." She tried to see past him into the house. No sign of Marianne. But she could be anywhere.

"The furniture was delivered this afternoon. It looks great."

He was mentioning the furniture, but not a word about the mother of his twins popping up out of thin air? "Um…that's good."

"Want to see?" His expression shifted from friendly to quizzical. "But maybe you're busy right now?"

"No. Not busy." He was acting so normal, she realized that Marianne hadn't gone to visit him after all.

She relaxed with the relief. The moment of reckoning had been postponed, and like a coward she was glad. Maybe, if she was really lucky, Marianne would decide to leave town without even bothering to visit Gavin and Tory.

Gavin held the door for her as she went inside. The house still smelled of paint, though the windows were open and a fan was running in the hall. The painting he'd bought at her store looked great in the foyer. As did the bench they'd found in Concord on the weekend.

"This fits perfectly." She ran a hand over the light maple surface.

"Yeah. I'm pretty happy with it. Check out the stools we got for the kitchen."

Tory was sitting on one, eating a snack of cheese and apple slices. "Hi, Allison!"

Allison gave her a hug. "The stools do look nice," she said to Gavin. The leather had been a smart choice and would be practical for cleanups, too.

"Come see the bookshelves we bought for the living room."

Gavin led her to the big room they'd only finished painting the night before. The new shelves looked like built-ins, and he'd already loaded half of them with books.

"Everything's coming together so well. You're definitely going to be ready for your family to arrive on Tory's birthday."

"Thanks to you."

Gavin moved closer. On the pretext of straightening the cushions on the sofa, she shifted away.

"Is something wrong?"

She really should tell him Marianne was in town. Even though the other woman hadn't bothered to look him up, he would still want to know.

The words, however, just wouldn't come.

Then, as if reading her mind, he said, "You'll never guess who called me today."

Her tongue thickened. Here it came. She tried to prepare herself. "Oh?"

"I had a response to that ad I placed in the *New England Chronicle*."

She almost cried with relief. "That's wonderful."

"Those draft plans for the cottage you saw last weekend? I think I'm going to have a chance to actually build it."

"I'm glad, Gavin. It'll make such a beautiful home. Your clients will be thrilled with it."

Gavin narrowed the distance between them again, trapping her between him and the sofa. Despite her worries, it was wonderful having him close.

"They'll be even happier if you agree to consult with me on the project. You'll be in charge of the kitchen design, bathrooms, color scheme and window coverings, all of that. What do you say?"

"It's an exciting opportunity."

"I think so, too. I already know we work well together."

"Does this mean you won't be accepting that opportunity with Jenkins Development?"

"That's right."

"Are you worried about not having a steady paycheck?"

"Not really. I'd rather take the risk and do something I love. Besides, I wasn't keen on working with your ex-fiancé."

"Oh?"

"I thought it might be a little awkward. Given that I was hoping you and I might start seeing one another."

She could feel her cheeks growing hot.

He touched a finger to her face. "Am I moving too fast?"

"No," she said quickly. She had no doubt that this was what she wanted, too.

"That's good. Because I've got more good news."

"I'm not sure I can handle more." Her knees were already feeling a little weak.

"Tory's made a friend at school."

It wasn't what she'd expected, but she was happy to hear it. "Gavin, that's wonderful."

"I think so, too. Dara was over for a little while today, and she's invited Tory to go to her house tomorrow."

"Wow. Does Tory want to go?"

"Amazingly, she does."

"I'm glad." She knew this was a big step for Tory.

"But here's the interesting thing. Dara's mom is going to pick them both up after school. Tory won't be coming home until five." He stopped. Raised an eyebrow. "So I was hoping you and I could skip out for a few hours in the afternoon. Have our first official date."

Her pulse sped up at the idea. "I like the sound of that."

"I'd rather take you out for dinner and have an entire evening together. But as a single father, that just isn't realistic right now. Not until Tory's secure enough to stay with a sitter."

"I understand," she assured him, but his comment about being a single father brought back the guilt she'd been suffering from earlier. She knew she should tell him about Marianne. But Gavin was looking at her as if she was the only woman in the world who mattered to him, and mentioning Marianne right now would wreck everything. Would it be so wrong to wait at least until after they'd had their date?

"What time should I be ready tomorrow?" she asked.

CHAPTER THIRTEEN

THE NEXT DAY Gavin showed up at Allison's door at one o'clock, as they'd agreed. They had reservations for lunch, but the moment their eyes met Allison knew they would be canceling them.

He pulled her into his arms and kissed her deeply. Then he eased back to look at her. "Your skin is as golden as the sunshine. And it tastes like crisp autumn air."

"Mmm. Poetic."

"What I meant to say was, you look really hot in that dress."

She laughed, then twined her arms around his neck. He didn't need more of an invitation. His next kiss was searing, and she felt his arms gently pressing her closer as they moved inside. He closed the door with his foot, then guided her to the sofa.

Gavin branded every square inch of her face and her neck with his kisses. He told her about all the other places he intended to kiss. Places that should have been off-limits, but weren't any longer.

"Make love to me," she pleaded at last.

"I am, sweetheart." He continued the kisses, the touching, the stroking. She was nothing but a puddle on the sofa cushions when he finally helped her to her feet and led her to the bedroom.

THEY DID MAKE IT out for lunch, about two hours late, to the nicest restaurant in town, where they were shown to a small, square table by the window. Rather than sit across from her, Gavin chose the seat to her left.

"You can't see the view from there," she said. The sun was bright today and the water sparkled like golden champagne.

Gavin just looked at her and smiled, as if to say he could see what he wanted to see. She felt the effect of that smile down to her pink-polished toes.

"Tell me why you decided to become an architect?" She needed him to talk, because otherwise all she would think about was how wonderful it had felt to make love with him.

And then she'd want to go home and do it again.

He reached over and caressed her hand. "You sure you want to talk shop?"

She nodded.

"Why I became an architect? It was probably because of a book of my father's on rural architecture by Andrew Jackson Downing. Ever heard of him?"

"The name is familiar. I think he was mentioned in one of my college courses."

"Downing talked about the need for an architect to stamp both feeling and imagination onto his work…"

As he talked, he continued to stroke her hand. She tried to concentrate on his words and not wish that he was touching the rest of her body right now, too.

"And the importance of truthfulness in material really hit home, as well." He cleared his throat. "Are you listening?"

"You have my undivided attention."

"Somehow I don't think so." He let go of her hand. "You're not regretting what just happened, are you?"

"Far from it. In fact…" She put a hand suggestively on the top button of her dress and had the satisfaction of seeing him shift uncomfortably in his chair.

"You know, we could skip the food part of

this date," he said quickly. "I hear the halibut is highly overrated."

She glanced at her watch. They had another hour before he was supposed to pick up Tory from Dara's house. "Why don't we do that?"

They were both rising from their chairs when the door to the restaurant opened and Allison's worst fears were realized.

Gavin saw her, too.

"Marianne?" He sounded as if he had seen a ghost. Allison only wished that he had.

WAS HE HALLUCINATING? Gavin stared at the woman who'd just entered the restaurant. She was walking toward him, as casually as if they saw each other every day.

"Marianne?"

She was real, and beautiful as ever, dressed in tattered jeans and a shrunken T-shirt that exposed her almost skeletal clavicle.

He'd imagined her coming back into his life so many times but never like this, so cavalierly and so unexpected. Not to mention, in the middle of the first date he'd had in ages.

Belatedly, he glanced at Allison. Her face had gone completely white and her lips were compressed, as if she was struggling not to say something unpleasant.

He wanted to reassure her. But he couldn't handle anything beyond Marianne's appearance at the moment. Where had she come from? How had she managed to show up now, of all times?

"Hi, Gavin. Allison." Marianne's cool gaze slipped from him to Allison, then back to him. "You look so surprised."

"It's been a lot of years."

"I heard you were looking for me."

"I was, but I had no idea you were in town."

"I arrived yesterday." She glanced back at Allison. "Didn't she tell you?"

Allison had known Marianne was in town? As Gavin looked at her to confirm this, a dark blush bloomed on Allison's face.

Why the hell hadn't she told him? He stared into her eyes, hoping she would volunteer an answer, and she slowly lowered her gaze.

"I should get back to the store."

What? She was just going to take off without saying anything more than that? Too stunned to argue, he watched her leave.

Marianne moved closer and put a hand on his

arm. He was surprised to see that her nails were stained with what looked like paint.

"Can we talk?" she asked.

"Of course." But not here. Good thing the restaurant was all but deserted at this hour. They'd already provided enough drama for the staff. "Let's go to my house."

Marianne didn't have a car, so he drove her in his. Her gaze took in the single booster seat in the back. She seemed about to ask a question, but in the end she sat silently, hands folded in her lap.

When he pulled into the driveway, Marianne stared out at the house. "I still can't believe you live here."

"There aren't that many family homes to choose from in Squam Lake. This one happened to be on the market." That wasn't the whole story, but he wasn't in the mood to reveal his deeper motivations at the moment.

He got out to open Marianne's door for her. As she stepped onto the driveway, he glanced at Allison's house, wondering if she'd gone there or back to the store.

Just thinking about her made his anger rise. He had to talk to her about this. To find out why she hadn't seen fit to tell him that Marianne was in town.

But that conversation would have to wait.

"This way," he said, leading Marianne up to the front door. They passed through the entry where she paused to look at the painting, and then headed down the hall to the kitchen.

Marianne stopped and looked around. "You're fixing the place up. It looks great."

"We're not done yet."

"We?"

"The job was too big to tackle alone," he said, avoiding a direct answer. He couldn't think about Allison right now, let alone talk about her. Something he hadn't wanted to acknowledge was eating at him. There'd been hurt in her eyes in that moment before she'd left the restaurant.

Why?

Shouldn't he be the one who felt betrayed?

"Let's go upstairs to my office. It's one of the few rooms that isn't a mess right now." He led Marianne through the house she'd grown up in. For the first time, his decision to buy this place struck him as bizarre. Obviously, Marianne felt the same way.

"This is so surreal." On the second floor she

stopped in front of Tory's room. The door was open, but she didn't step inside. "This used to be my room."

"Allison told me."

"She's the one who's helping you decorate, right?"

He nodded.

"Interesting." Marianne turned from Tory's room to his office. "This was my mother's sewing room when I was growing up. Not that I remember her doing much sewing."

She entered the room tentatively and seemed nervous when he closed the door behind them. He watched as she positioned herself next to the window.

"So, how are the girls?"

Girls. She didn't know. *How could she not know?* "I thought you would have heard."

"What?" She wrapped her arms around her waist. Everything about her seemed so thin and delicate. Had she always been this way? He couldn't remember.

"There was an accident, Marianne. It happened more than a year ago."

"What?" she asked again, sharply this time.

"Sam was run over by a motorcycle on the way

home from school. I was holding her hand, but she pulled away and ran into the street." His facial muscles were so tight he could hardly finish telling her. "She darted between two parked cars. The driver of the motorcycle never saw her coming."

Marianne shook her head. "No."

She started to tremble. Gavin rolled his desk chair over to her. "Sit down."

She crumpled into the seat and he put his hands on her thin shoulders.

"You wouldn't let that happen. You were such a good father."

Her words were both a comfort and an indictment. Yes, he'd been a good father. Everyone told him so. But his daughter had died on his watch.

"I was there, holding her hand. She just slipped out of my grasp. I don't know how she did it. I've been over that day so many times in my mind."

He'd wanted this for a long time. A chance to talk about what had happened with the one person who would understand, the mother of his children.

But Marianne's expression offered him no sympathy for his pain. Her eyes were oddly blank. "I knew I shouldn't have had them."

"Don't. How can you say that? We still have

Tory. And I wouldn't give up the years we had with Sam for anything."

"The years *you* had, Gavin."

He had thought the same thing, though he hadn't said it. He didn't want to blame her. Didn't want her to suffer the way he had.

But now that the first shock was passing, he could see that Marianne didn't seem to be suffering. At least not in any way that he recognized.

"If you didn't know about Sam, then why did you want to see me? Do you want to be a part of Tory's life now? Is that it?"

Marianne didn't answer at first. She turned her head to look out the window, but her eyes didn't focus. She seemed to be summoning her energy before giving him an answer. Finally, she looked back at him.

"I'm sick, Gavin. I need your help."

As soon as she'd left the restaurant, Allison went back to her shop. She didn't know where else to go. Certainly not home, to the house right next to Gavin's. She imagined that was where he'd take Marianne. They would have a talk, she supposed, though she hadn't stayed in the restaurant long enough to find out.

The condemnation on Gavin's face when he'd found out she hadn't told him Marianne was in town had been enough to make her want to leave.

Let him think the worst of her. She couldn't really blame him—she should have told him about Marianne. Instead, she'd tried to pretend the other woman didn't exist. As if ignoring a problem would make it go away.

Not a smart plan.

"What's wrong, dear?" Gertie asked during a lull in business. "Didn't the date go well?"

Allison wasn't ready to talk about what had happened. "It was fine, Gertie. Thanks for covering for me.

"Why don't you leave early in exchange. I expect business will be slow now until closing."

It wouldn't be slow, and Gertie knew it. But she also must have understood that Allison needed to be alone. So she nodded and collected her purse. On the way out the door, she gave Allison a hug. "Call me, if you want to talk."

Allison promised she would. Once Gertie was gone, she started tidying things up. It seemed hardly any time had passed at all before her father called her.

"I heard about what happened."

Small towns. Why did she like them, again?

"I warned you not to date that man."

"Dad…"

"The last thing I wanted was to see you hurt again."

Hurt? Did he know something she didn't? She closed her mind to an unbidden vision of Marianne and Gavin locked in an embrace in the restaurant where she'd left them. She wouldn't assume the worst until she'd talked to Gavin.

After all, he'd just made love to *her,* not Marianne. He wasn't the sort of man who would do that if it didn't mean something.

"Dad, I wasn't hurt before and I'm not hurt this time, either. Look, we'll discuss this at dinner tonight."

"Actually, I need to cancel for tonight. In fact, the entire week doesn't look good."

This was not like her father. "Are you sick?"

"I'm fine. Something's come up, that's all. Okay if I see you next week?"

"Sure, Dad." She decided against asking for details. Maybe her father had a date, too. After all these years without her mother, that would be wonderful.

She had a flurry of customers to deal with

after she hung up and for a while she was able to forget her worries. Just before closing, a tourist from Iowa walked in looking for a piece of art to take with her as a souvenir of her New England trip. She stopped in front of Marianne's big piece.

"This is very good."

"Yes, it is."

The tourist stood there a long time, considering, before finally deciding against it and leaving.

Once she was gone, Allison studied Marianne's latest—violent swirls of red, with dashes of orange and jabs of black. It was as if she'd wrestled those colors onto the canvas. Who would want a painting like that in her home? She wasn't surprised the woman from Iowa had decided against it.

After moving the painting farther back in the store, she tried to turn her attention to paperwork. At nine o'clock, Allison closed down the computer and locked the shop. She walked home in the dark, along familiar streets, with the crunch of leaves beneath her shoes.

As she rounded the corner onto Robin Crescent Gavin happened to emerge from his backyard, carrying a big orange garbage bag stuffed with leaves.

GAVIN'S FIRST INSTINCT when he saw Allison was to draw her into his arms. The impulse was quickly overcome with remembered anger, however. He set down the bag of leaves he'd been carrying at the curb.

"Where's Tory?"

"Inside, asleep." He couldn't contain himself any longer. "Why didn't you tell me Marianne was in town?"

"I should have. I'm sorry."

The simple apology caught him off guard. "Where did you see her? Did she come to your house?"

"No. She dropped off one of her paintings at the store."

"Paintings?"

"Marianne is an artist."

"She is?" He pictured her hands, flecked with paint. So that explained that.

"Professionally she's known simply as Anna. That's how she signs all her work. I've been carrying her pieces at the store for years."

He felt overwhelmed by the obviousness of it all. "I almost bought one of them."

"Yes."

"How long has she painted?"

"A long time. Before she met you."

"I never knew."

"You said she didn't talk about her work," she recalled.

"No. When I asked about her career, she avoided a straight answer. She implied it was too boring to talk about. Even after we found out she was pregnant and she moved in with me, I didn't see any clues. She arrived with just one big suitcase and a couple of cardboard boxes. I don't remember seeing any painting supplies."

"Marianne has always been extremely private about her art."

"When I met her…" Something else was clicking into place for him. "Holy cow. That was *her* art show."

"She did tell me she was having some success in Hartford," Allison recalled. "I couldn't figure out why she just seemed to stop painting all of a sudden. Now I know it must have been the twins."

Marianne had been building a career as an artist? No wonder she'd felt so trapped at home with the babies. "She never told me what she was giving up. If she had, I would have found a way to make it work."

"I'm not sure you could have. Marianne has

always needed a lot of time and isolation in order to paint. Recently, she's been living and working out of her trailer, and it sounds like she's been productive. Now she wants my help to sell the paintings. She seems rather desperate for money."

Yes. And now he knew why. But he didn't say anything about that yet. "I still don't understand why you didn't talk to me after she showed up at your store."

Allison hugged the case she'd been carrying to her chest, as if it gave her some sort of strength or protection. "I don't have a good excuse, Gavin. But I've already apologized. I can't say anything beyond that."

"Where has she been staying? Not with you, I assume?"

"No. Not with me. I don't know where else she would go, though. Maybe one of the inns."

He doubted if Marianne had money for that. "What if Marianne hadn't found me at the restaurant? Would you ever have told me about her?"

"I would have."

"That's hard for me to believe right now."

She sighed. "Okay, the real reason is that I was

insecure. Things were going so well between us. When Marianne showed up at the store, I was afraid she was going to ruin things."

He didn't pretend not to understand what she meant. He hadn't known, himself, how he would feel when he saw Marianne again. Part of him had wondered if he would still be susceptible to her mysterious allure.

"It wasn't easy being Marianne's friend," Allison said softly. "You know how beautiful she is. Every guy she meets falls in love with her. But when we were teenagers, the only ones she ever seemed interested in were the ones that *I* liked. This is going to sound juvenile, but I was afraid that if Marianne knew I was seeing you, she'd try to win you back."

"The way I felt about you this afternoon when we made love… That hasn't changed."

She didn't look reassured. "Maybe not. But something has."

"Not between you and me," he insisted, wanting it to be true. "But Marianne did have something to tell me this afternoon that's going to affect both of us."

"I knew it," Allison said softly.

"It's not what you think."

"She wants to get back with you."

"No," he insisted. "That isn't it at all. She's sick, and she needs me to help take care of her."

ALLISON TOOK A MOMENT to let his words sink in. She hadn't seen this coming. Maybe she should have. With Marianne, something always happened that allowed her to seize center stage when the focus had drifted away from her. A switch-about to turn herself from the bad guy into an object of sympathy.

Marianne had walked out on the man who loved her and their children. Instead of blaming her for that, Gavin was now going to feel sorry for her.

Stop it, Allison told herself. She had reasons to resent Marianne, but this was going too far. No one wanted to be sick.

Besides, what if it was serious?

"I noticed how thin she was," she admitted. "What's wrong?"

"She hasn't been feeling well for a long time. She went to several different doctors, but they had trouble agreeing on a diagnosis." Gavin rubbed a hand over the side of his face. He looked tired and careworn.

It simply wasn't fair. He'd been through so much. He had his own daughter to worry about.

And now Marianne was dumping this on his lap.

Allison couldn't help resenting her for it. "How long has she been feeling this way?"

"Since last winter, apparently. Her trailer doesn't sound like it's the warmest. She started having trouble sleeping, which led to fatigue and body aches. She was deep into her work and tried to ignore the symptoms at first."

Allison had seen Marianne when she was submerged in the creative process. She would paint for days, forgetting to eat and sleeping only when she was absolutely exhausted. "She was probably driving herself too hard."

"That's what she thought, initially. But then, she finished what she was working on and started to pay some attention to her health. The symptoms didn't go away. Finally, she went to see a doctor, and then another and another. Her current physician thinks she has fibromyalgia. Have you heard of that?"

"One of my regular customers suffers from it. She has for years. It took the doctors a long time to figure out what was wrong with her, though."

"What is it, exactly? I haven't had a chance to do any research yet. I was planning to look on the Internet tonight.

"Fatigue and muscle pain are the main symptoms. But they can be managed. My customer lives a fairly normal life."

"Hopefully one day Marianne will get to that point."

Allison said nothing. She couldn't help but feel skeptical about the whole thing. If Marianne had wanted to pick a disease to fake, she couldn't have chosen a better one. Fibromyalgia was notoriously difficult to diagnose. And the symptoms were constantly changing.

"Hopefully, she will," she agreed, keeping her doubts to herself. "But what does that have to do with you?" How, exactly, did Marianne expect him to take care of her?

"Her doctor has prescribed a treatment plan, but she can't live in her trailer this winter. Nor can she afford a house in town."

"No." She looked at him, begging him with her eyes to tell her she was wrong. She knew what he was going to say, just *knew* it. But she had to hear the words from him.

"She's moving in tomorrow."

"Gavin…"

He swallowed. Looked away. "She doesn't have anyone else to turn to."

"She walked out on you."

"She's Tory's mother."

"She hasn't acted like one."

"I know. Damn it, I do know that. But this could be Tory's chance to get to know her. Maybe they'll find a connection. And that connection could be the thing to save both of them."

"But what about us?"

"Like I said earlier, this doesn't change how I feel about you."

Maybe not yet it didn't. But with Marianne living under the same roof with him, how long would it take?

Gavin rested a hand on her shoulder. "I know it's a lot to ask, but I was hoping this wouldn't change how you feel about me, either."

Of course it didn't. It only made her admire him more. But at the same time she wanted to kick him. This was going to be torture for her. Couldn't he understand that?

"If I can just help her get through the winter, maybe she'll be well enough to move back to the trailer in the spring."

So Marianne was going to live with him for six whole months? "I don't know, Gavin. It might help if you would answer one question for me. Are you helping Marianne out of duty alone?"

His expression grew cautious. "What do you mean?"

"You said that Tory and Marianne might develop a connection. What about you and Marianne?"

Gavin looked away from her and let out a heavy sigh. "That doesn't seem likely."

"But you aren't ruling it out?"

"She's the mother of my child. That's all that's behind this, I swear."

Suddenly, it seemed like a lot to Allison. She realized, then, that her father's warning had been right on. Marianne, once again, held all the cards.

"Asking for our relationship to continue is too much, isn't it?" Gavin said softly.

When she didn't respond, he continued. "I'm sorry I even put you in this position. It isn't fair. I see that now. You deserve more from a man than what I'm offering. You deserve…everything."

He was being honorable and she hated it. Marianne wasn't worthy of his loyalty. Couldn't he see that?

"You deserve more, too, Gavin."

"Marianne didn't want to have the babies. I talked her into it. This is all on my head. Don't think of me as some kind of martyr—it's just the right thing to do. I owe her."

CHAPTER FOURTEEN

AFTER HIS CONVERSATION with Allison, Gavin knew it would be a long while before he'd be able to sleep. First he checked on Tory, and then he went to the kitchen to pour himself his second scotch of the evening. Out on the deck, he sipped it slowly.

Wispy clouds seemed to cling to the half-moon. The night air had developed a bite. He held the cold at bay with another taste of the scotch. When the drink was finished and he still felt empty and alone, he phoned his brother.

"Hey, Matt. How are you doing?"

"Not great. I just phoned my son and had a most unsatisfactory conversation. I was trying to set up something fun for next weekend. But he has a birthday party sleepover on Saturday and soccer on Sunday. Won't be much time left after that."

"You can watch his game," Gavin suggested. "Cook dinner together afterward. Doing every-day chores with your kids is a great way to bond."

"Not the way I cook. How about you? What's going on there?"

"More than you can imagine. Marianne showed up today."

"You're kidding me."

"She's always had a terrible sense of timing. Things were just starting to go well with me and Allison."

"I knew it."

"Yeah, well, Marianne informed me today that she's sick."

"I take it we're not talking about flu or a cold?"

"No—it's serious. Fibromyalgia."

"Let me guess. She came to you looking for sympathy?"

"Something like that."

"Are you sure it isn't a con?"

"You should see her. She's so thin and weak-looking."

"Okay, so she's telling the truth and she has fibromyalgia. But what's her poor health to do with you?"

"She's too ill to live on her own."

"You're not suggesting…"

"She wants to move in with me and Tory."

"You're not going to let her, right? Tell me you aren't that stupid."

"Marianne and I aren't getting back together. I'm just letting her stay here." When his brother said nothing, Gavin added, "She has no one else. Her mother died years ago and her dad was never around. Besides, it'll give Tory a chance to get to know her mother."

"And you think that's a good thing? Before Sam died, the three of you were doing just fine without Marianne."

"That was then."

Matt's voice softened. "Life will never be the same without Sam. But Tory is starting to heal. You both are. You were smart to make this move. But letting Marianne shack up there? Not so smart."

"You don't know that."

"Tory was just a baby when Marianne left. She won't remember her."

"There's more to the bond between mother and child than that."

"Maybe with most mothers and their children." Matt's tone grew harder. "Face it, Gavin.

Marianne doesn't have any maternal urges— she's too damn focused on herself."

Gavin knew Matt had his reasons to be cynical. "Priorities change as you get older. And there's nothing like a chronic illness to teach you what's really important in life."

"I suppose it's possible she's changed." Matt didn't sound convinced. "But what about Allison? What happens to the two of you, if Marianne moves in?"

"What do you think?"

"I guess I'd be pissed if I were her."

"That pretty much sums it up. I can't expect someone like Allison…" He stopped. It was too painful to continue. When he thought of how bright his future had looked yesterday. And how bleak today.

It wasn't fair to Marianne for him to think this way. He couldn't resent her for coming between Allison and him. It wasn't her fault she was sick.

"In my opinion, you should show Marianne the door. I know you're too noble to do that. But it's what you ought to do. Now I'm going to bed. You do the same. And think about what I said, okay?"

ALLISON DUMPED HER BAG in the house and tried to take her mind off Gavin with some chores. She ended up out on the front porch, where she finally nailed that loose board back into place. When she was done, she sat back on her haunches and looked over at Gavin's.

Throughout that last painful conversation with him, Allison's chest had felt tight. As she'd watched him walk away from her, she'd tried to remember if she'd ever felt this miserable before. Certainly breaking up with Tyler hadn't been this hard.

Her parents' divorce. That had come close. She'd been an adult, but it had still been a shock. She'd never known her parents to fight—except, sometimes, about Marianne.

She got up from the porch and went back inside, determined not to look at his house one more time. She'd only known Gavin since August. This shouldn't be so hard. And yet it was. This weekend, she'd finally realized the truth.

She was in love with him.

Damn Marianne for showing up now, at the worst possible time. Allison was sorry she was sick, but surely she had had other options beyond appealing to Gavin's sense of honor and responsibility.

In the end, Allison realized that she had to leave the house or she'd lose it. She tried calling her father, but there was no answer. It was past ten and he didn't usually go to bed until late. Maybe he was working in his shop.

She decided to drive by and check. Even if he was out, just being in the house she'd grown up in would be a comfort. She decided to take some bananas with her—her father loved banana loaf. She'd make a treat for him while she was waiting for him to get home.

Over the ten minutes it took to drive to the other side of town, Allison was already feeling better. She could hear music as she got out of the car. That was good. She wondered if he simply hadn't heard the phone when she'd called. Maybe the receiver needed recharging. He often forgot to put it back in the cradle.

She ran up the steps and knocked at the door as a courtesy, before trying the handle. Her dad only locked the place when he was going out. She walked inside.

"Dad?"

She heard noises in the kitchen. It sounded

like he was doing dishes. Then she heard a woman's voice.

Oh, dear. Suddenly, she remembered her earlier suspicion that her father might have started to date. She stopped where she was. "Dad? It's me, Allison."

"Hi, Allie." He sounded strained. A moment later she understood why. He stepped into the living room, carrying a dishrag.

Right behind him was Marianne.

CHAPTER FIFTEEN

"WHAT IS SHE DOING HERE?" Allison didn't care that she sounded like a spoiled child. She felt betrayed. She dropped the bananas on a nearby table. "How long has she been here?"

Her father took her arm and led her to his study. "What is the matter with you? You haven't behaved this way since you were six."

"But, Dad…" As he closed the door, she realized she wasn't being fair to him. He didn't know how she felt about Gavin—or how Marianne had manipulated that situation. She tried to speak more calmly. "Why is she here, Dad? Has she been staying with you?"

"Why wouldn't she come to see me? I was her teacher. And a good friend of her mother's."

Allison let his words sink in.

Marianne's mother had taught in the same school as her father. She'd been the home economics teacher, which was kind of funny when you considered the fact that she'd never managed to make a proper home for her own daughter.

She'd always been too busy partying. Allison had never been privy to the exact details. She hadn't wanted to know. If Marianne had any idea where her mother spent her free time, she'd never let on.

An ugly suspicion was forming now, as Allison considered possibilities that would have destroyed her as a child.

"Just how good was the friendship between you and Marianne's mother?"

Her father glared at her. "You have no right to ask that question. I was a good husband and a good father."

Yes, he had been. But maybe not always? The possibility that she might have just stumbled on the reason for her parents' divorce left her wordless.

"Allison, I can see what you're thinking and I'm warning you right now. You have no right to question me about this—I'm your father and I love you. You've always been able to count on me, and that's never going to change."

She sank into his chair, her head dropping into her hands. His words penetrated slowly.

He was right about one thing. She'd always been able to count on him. Which was why finding Marianne here hurt so much. "Why the secrecy? Obviously you canceled our dinners because Marianne was staying with you. Why didn't you tell me?"

"She asked me not to. Now I understand why. You've always been jealous of her." He shook his head, his eyes sad. "She didn't grow up with your advantages."

The old lecture. Allison was so tired of hearing it. "She had advantages of her own. Beauty. Talent. Money." Had he forgotten that Marianne had been born into one of the richest families in town?

"The McLaughlin money was gone by the time her grandfather died. All that was left was the house. Besides, what good is money when you don't have a stable family life? You know how Marianne lived. The only decent meals she ate were at our place. I would have hoped for more compassion from you." He picked up a book from his desk, then set it down again. "She's sick, you know."

Allison had to drop her gaze. "I heard."

"Well, then?" He reached out a hand to her and squeezed her arm. "She won't be here much longer. Let's go have a cup of coffee together and a little conversation. Try to remember the fun you had together when you were girls."

HER FATHER WAS PARTLY RIGHT. She and Marianne had shared some good times together, working on their art and canoeing and swimming in the lake. But there had been unpleasant times, too. Allison realized she couldn't tell him about those now, just as she couldn't have when she was a young girl. In her father's eyes, she was the one with all the advantages.

And maybe he was right about that. She'd grown up with a mother and father who loved her and who were always there for her.

Marianne hadn't had that.

In the kitchen, the three of them sat around the table with their mugs of coffee and Allison did her best to be pleasant and civil. Mostly, they talked about prospects for selling Marianne's paintings. There was an opportunity for a show in November at a gallery in Concord and Marianne was weighing the pros and cons.

Then the phone rang and her father got up to take the call in his study.

Allison studied Marianne's face. Illness suited

her. Only someone with flawless skin could look as good as she did, deathly pale. Her gauntness simply emphasized her high cheekbones. And though her lips had almost no color, they were still full, still that pretty cupid shape.

Allison knew she ought to keep quiet until her father returned, but after a long, silent minute, she couldn't help herself. "So you're moving in with Gavin and Tory tomorrow?"

At first, Marianne said nothing. Then she cocked her head to one side. "You're in love with him, aren't you?"

Damn her. She knew. Of course she knew. Allison clenched her teeth and let her anger sink into the pit of her stomach, waiting until it was under control before she dared to speak.

"We've only known each other since August." She got up from the table to rinse her mug and place it in the dishwasher.

"That doesn't matter. You still love him." Marianne said this as if she'd just figured it out. But she'd known all along. She gave Allison a smile that was all innocence.

Allison wasn't fooled. She also knew she couldn't be in the same room as this woman for one minute longer.

"I just remembered something I need to do. Tell my father goodbye for me, would you?"

IT WAS DÉJÀ VU FOR Gavin when Marianne showed up on his doorstep at noon the next day with a suitcase and two cardboard boxes. She'd had exactly the same luggage the day she'd moved in with him in Hartford, shortly after discovering she was pregnant. He'd been surprised, then, by how little she owned. When she'd moved out a year and a half later she had taken even less than she'd arrived with.

Traveling light was Marianne's style.

"How are you feeling?" He'd never seen anyone with skin so pale. Her hair was in a ponytail and the style emphasized the thinness of her face. She swayed slightly when she tried to pick up her suitcase. He took it from her.

"You didn't carry all this?"

"I got a lift."

Who gave her the ride? He waited, but she didn't offer any additional information. He still didn't know where she'd been staying while she was in Squam Lake. It hardly seemed to matter now.

"Go in and sit down. I'll bring your stuff."

He tried not to look over at Allison's place as he heaved the boxes over the threshold. But he couldn't stop himself.

That morning she'd decorated for Halloween. She had a scarecrow sitting in the wicker rocker on her porch and an attractive display of pumpkins and other colorful vegetables that looked like mutilated squash. Tory had been delighted at the sight on her way to school that morning. He supposed he'd have to get some pumpkins, too, and decorate.

The prospect depressed him, especially since he knew that if this had been one week earlier, he and Tory would have had a blast preparing for Halloween with Allison.

He made three trips from the front landing to the spare bedroom. When he returned to the main floor, he found Marianne prowling in the kitchen, opening drawers randomly and peering at the contents.

He tried not to feel resentment. He'd invited her to stay. She had every right to be in this room.

"Are you hungry?"

"Not really. It's just weird to see the old place looking so different." She opened the top cupboard next to the stove where he kept all his canned goods. "We never had much food in the house when I was a kid."

Being reminded of her tough childhood helped him muster some sympathy for her. "We need to talk. Tory will be home from school in a few hours."

"Yeah?" Marianne pulled out a box of cookies. She brought them to the table and sat down to eat one.

"As you can imagine, she's had a hard time since Sam died. We both have," he acknowledged. "We're just starting to get back on our feet and I don't want to risk upsetting her."

Marianne stopped chewing. "You think my moving in is going to upset her?"

"It might. So for now I think we should just say that you're an old friend of mine, staying at the house for a little rest."

"You don't want to tell her I'm her mother?"

"Tory's been seeing a grief counselor. I called her yesterday and explained the situation. She advised against springing too much on Tory, too fast. Let her get to know you first, without any pressure."

With luck, nature would take its course after that.

ON THE WALK HOME from school, Tory was full of chatter about a policeman who had been in to visit her class. Normally, Gavin gave his daughter his undivided attention, but today his mind was preoccupied. He didn't know how Tory was going to react when she encountered Marianne in their home.

Though it had been most of her life, was it possible that she would somehow still recognize her mother? After all, there was that photograph of Marianne in her bedroom.

He'd moved himself and his daughter to Squam Lake hoping for this exact outcome—to reunite his daughter with her mother. But now that it was about to happen, he was full of doubt.

Over the years, he'd forgotten just how self-absorbed Marianne could be. How cool and distant. It was highly unlikely that this woman was going to help fill the void that Sam's passing had left in Tory's life.

Still, he didn't regret opening his home to her. Regardless of her faults, Marianne was Tory's mother, and he wanted his daughter to have a chance to get to know her.

Who knew? Maybe a miracle would happen.

Maybe spending time with Tory would bring out Marianne's latent maternal side.

As they rounded the corner to Robin Crescent, Tory pointed to Allison's house. "Daddy, I want to see the scarecrow."

Tory had no idea, of course, that her father's relationship with Allison had changed. Her fondness for their next-door neighbor was going to make the next few months extremely awkward.

His best hope was to distract her.

"Maybe later, Tory. First I want you to meet that new lady I was telling you about."

"Your sick friend?"

He could tell she was a little apprehensive about the situation. He wished there was something he could say to reassure her—*she's really nice* or *you're going to like her.* But he had his doubts on both those scores, and he wasn't in the habit of lying to his daughter.

They went in the front entrance, checking out the main floor before they found Marianne on the back deck. She was staring out at the lake pensively, but she put on a smile at the sight of her daughter.

"Hey, Tory, it's nice to meet you."

"This is…" Gavin hesitated. The name was

going to be a dead giveaway. Why hadn't he thought of this sooner?

"Anna," Marianne said smoothly, using the name she signed on her paintings. "You can call me Anna."

Tory said hello quietly, hanging back near her father. Gavin tried not to be discouraged by her initial response. He reminded himself that she hadn't taken to Allison right away, either.

Gavin had to give Marianne credit. She made an effort to connect with Tory, asking to see her room and then showing genuine interest in the art projects from school that were displayed on the fridge.

"Hey, she's talented," she murmured to Gavin.

Gavin looked at the pictures with fresh eyes, realizing he'd taken his daughter's gift for drawing and coloring as a given.

Though Marianne had never been much of a cook, she did her best to be helpful in the kitchen that evening. She washed and chopped vegetables for Gavin, set the table and cleaned up after the meal.

By Tory's bath time, however, it was obvious Marianne had exhausted herself. She went to bed early, leaving Gavin and Tory to go through the usual bedtime routine alone. As he was tucking her under the covers, Tory asked, "Why is she staying here, Daddy?"

It was a question he'd been asking himself all night. Though Marianne was doing her best, he'd found just having her around exhausting. Allison seemed to add energy when she was here. Marianne sucked it all up.

"I already explained, Tory. She's a friend and she's not feeling well right now. She needs a place to stay for a while." He brushed Tory's dark hair away from her forehead. She was so like her mother in appearance. And now he realized they shared an artistic sensibility, as well. It had to be right that he was giving them this opportunity to get to know each other. To develop a bond.

Even if it meant he'd forfeited his chance with Allison for it to happen?

That part he wasn't nearly as sure about.

THE NIGHT AFTER her impromptu visit to her father's, Allison slept fitfully. She dreamed about the art competition she'd entered when she was in grade school. Marianne had encouraged her to submit one of her drawings.

"Why? Yours are better."

"I don't have time to paint anything right

now," Marianne had said. "But you've already got something to enter. You should go ahead and do it."

Allison had let her talk her into it. Then, on the day of the judging, she'd seen the first-prize ribbon attached to one of Marianne's paintings.

"I thought you said you weren't going to enter?"

"I changed my mind."

Allison woke up, feeling an anger she knew had nothing to do with a child's disappointment about a silly art competition. She remembered what her father had said that long-ago night, when she'd shared the story at the dinner table. He'd given her a talk about not being a sore loser, and reminded her—for the hundredth time—how fortunate she was compared to Marianne.

Maybe there was more than compassion behind his concern for Marianne. Maybe there was also guilt?

Allison went to work, more troubled than ever by her new suspicion about her dad and Marianne's mother. An extramarital affair, ending with an illegitimate child, seemed too *Desperate Housewives* for her family.

But it would explain a number of things.

Like her father's feeling of responsibility for Marianne's well-being.

And her parents' divorce.

Only why would her mother have stayed with her dad for all those years? *For me,* Allison reasoned. After all, it had been right after she left home for design school that her mother had moved out.

Allison thought about confronting her father with her theory. But he'd already told her he didn't think any of this was her business.

She decided to phone her mom.

CHAPTER SIXTEEN

ALLISON WAITED until after work to place the call to New York. Her mom was happy to hear from her, until she broached the subject of Marianne.

"Guess who's back in town?"

"Who?" her mom asked cautiously.

"Marianne McLaughlin."

"Oh."

While her mother had never been fond of Marianne, she'd always been polite. At the same time, while Allison's dad had encouraged the friendship, her mom had often suggested she broaden her circle of friends.

So the cool tone of her mother's voice now didn't necessarily mean anything. Still, Allison was sure she was on the right track.

"Mom, I'd like to ask you something. It's about you and Dad and the divorce."

"What would you like to know, Allison?"

She exhaled heavily. So far, so good. "You guys never told me the reason you split up."

"We didn't want to risk putting you in the middle of the decision."

"And that's great. I do appreciate that." She had friends whose parents fought bitterly and spoke disparagingly of one another. How grateful she was that neither of her parents had stooped to such behavior.

"Your dad and I both love you very much."

"I know that, Mom. But I am an adult. And I have a feeling there are a few things I ought to know."

"Have you talked to your father about this?"

"Yes. He wasn't exactly forthcoming."

"Perhaps he has his reasons. Allison, maybe you should let this drop. There are some things you may be better off not knowing."

Allison had had enough of this. They were circling the subject with such caution. Both of them afraid to say the unspeakable. If she wanted to find out the truth, she was going to have to take the first step.

"Mom, is Dad Marianne's father?"

The silence on the other end of the line went on for so long that Allison was afraid she'd done the last thing she wanted to do and offended her mother.

"I'm sorry, Mom. If I'm wrong…"

"You're not wrong," her mother said in a quiet voice.

There was another long silence. This time Allison waited patiently, giving her mother time to gather her thoughts.

"I'm so sorry, Allison. I know how close you are to your father. I don't want you to think less of him because he had an affair. He was always a good father to you and I know he was tormented with guilt that he couldn't be the same to Marianne."

Allison was deeply touched by her mother's concern. "What about you, Mom? It must have been hard, having Marianne in our house all the time." A constant reminder of her husband's infidelity.

"But I didn't know, then. I didn't find out about the affair until much later."

"How did you find out?"

"Your grandmother's will. I guess your dad had confided in her."

"But Grandma left everything to me."

"Her business and the bulk of her money, yes. But there was a sum set aside for Marianne, too.

When I heard out about that, of course I figured out why. Your dad tried to deny it at first, but eventually he admitted the truth."

Suddenly, the enormity of having her suspicions confirmed hit her. Allison sank onto the cold tile floor.

She and Marianne were half sisters.

"Oh, Mom. This is unbelievable."

"I'm sorry," her mother said again.

But her mother had nothing to be sorry about. She'd been an innocent victim, just like Allison.

And Marianne.

The last thing she wanted was to feel sorry for Marianne, but suddenly she couldn't help but feel that way. Now that she knew the truth, she had to acknowledge her father had been right.

She had been the lucky one.

THAT WEEK Gavin carried on with the renovations on his own. Fortunately, most of the decisions already had been made, colors selected, products ordered. He hired someone to replace the flooring and painted every evening after he'd finished his work. Throughout the week, shipments of furniture and art that he and Allison had selected together were delivered.

Marianne watched all the activity from the sidelines. She spent most of her days either in bed or sitting out on the deck gazing at the lake.

She and Gavin didn't exactly avoid one another. But they didn't talk much, either.

At the end of the week, 11 Robin Crescent was looking good. Gavin realized it was time to plan the birthday party. But Tory, who had been complaining all week about missing Allison, wouldn't talk about it with him.

"I want Allison to help," she insisted.

Finally, one afternoon while Marianne was at a doctor's appointment, Gavin tried calling his neighbor. When there was no answer, he looked out the window to see if her car was in the driveway and spotted her on the lawn raking leaves.

"Come on, Tory," he called. "We're going outside."

AS SOON AS Tory saw Allison, she started to run. "Hey! Can we help you with the leaves?" Before Allison had time to answer, Tory hurled herself into the pile Allison had spent the past twenty minutes creating.

"Tory." Gavin caught up with her and scooped

her into his arms. "The idea is to put the leaves into bags, not fling them all over the yard again."

"I will. Put me down, Daddy. I promise I'll help the right way."

"You will?"

She nodded solemnly.

"Okay." He set her on the ground, then watched as she earnestly started to gather the leaves she'd just scattered.

He turned to Allison. "Sorry about that."

"No problem." He looked so good. She longed for those days when he would have wrapped his arms around her. So many times this week she'd had to stop herself from phoning him to tell him what she'd learned about Marianne.

But she'd restrained herself.

"Let me help with this mess," he offered.

He held out a hand for the rake, but she set it on the ground instead. "Do I look upset? I agree with Tory. It's awfully hard to resist jumping into a good pile of leaves. In fact… Watch out, Tory. Here I come."

She jumped right into the center, then sank back onto her butt. A moment later, Tory was in with her, tossing handfuls of colored leaves over her head.

Gavin looked at them, arms crossed over his chest. "You're both nuts."

Allison ignored him as she pretended to have lost Tory under the mound of leaves. "Where is that girl?" she muttered, tossing handfuls of leaves into the air before finally "finding" the little girl. Tory shrieked with pleasure.

"Now you hide," Tory commanded.

In the moment before she dove for cover, Allison noticed that Gavin had disappeared. The next time she saw him, he was crouched in front of them with a camera in his hands. By the time he'd taken several pictures, the game had grown old. Gavin exchanged his camera for the rake, and Allison and Tory held the garbage bags as he piled the leaves one last time. When they were finished, five large bags lined Allison's lawn.

"That was fun," Tory said. "But now I'm hungry."

Allison turned to Gavin. "I have cookies and some apples I bought at the farmers' market."

"Sounds perfect." He picked a leaf out of her hair and his hand brushed the side of her neck.

He couldn't know how that simple touch made her long for much, much more. But then she saw the way he was looking at her, and she realized he did know.

"Be careful, Gavin," she murmured. She'd spoken quietly so Tory wouldn't hear, but she needn't have worried. Tory had already sped ahead to the kitchen, making herself at home.

"I've missed you, Allison."

She glanced back at his house, to remind him who was still living there. He sighed, showing he got the message.

"Do you think we can go back to being just friends?" he asked her.

"We have to."

"Why?"

"Because we're neighbors. And also, for Tory's sake."

"You're right about that. She's missed you this week, too. I tried to get her to help me plan her birthday party, but she wouldn't do it without you."

There was satisfaction in knowing that. Allison had come to care deeply about Tory and it meant a lot to her that those feelings were reciprocated. "Speaking of Tory, we should go inside."

Gavin followed, and they took turns washing

their hands at the kitchen sink before perching on stools to eat their snack.

"Tory's birthday is next weekend," Gavin reminded them. "I've heard from Nick, and the whole family is coming."

"My cousins, too?"

"I'm sorry, Tory, but they can't make it. They have to stay in Hartford with Aunt Gillian. But Grandma and your uncles will be there. Plus, your new friends from school. We need to think about decorations and food and, of course, the birthday cake."

Gavin tried to make it sound like fun, but Allison could see all those decisions were over-whelming to Tory. "Maybe if you came up with a theme, it would be easier."

Tory looked mildly interested at that. "What's a theme?"

"A main idea. Like, if you wanted to use autumn as your theme, you could print your in-vitations on pieces of paper that look like leaves and you could carve pumpkins and have a cake in the shape of an apple…"

"Yes! Let's have a party like that one."

Allison saw the disappointment in Gavin's eyes. Too late, she realized her mistake. Tory was supposed to be learning to make her own decisions. He'd asked for her help with that, and here she was doing the opposite.

"That was just one example. You could have a rainbow theme or a princess party or cowboys or…anything you like. Anything that interests you."

But Tory wasn't about to change her mind now. A few minutes later, when the little girl excused herself to go to the bathroom, Allison apologized.

"I shouldn't have jumped in like that."

"To the leaves?" he teased.

She was glad he wasn't angry.

"I don't want her stressed about her birthday party of all things. We'll just keep working on the little decisions and work up to the bigger ones." He tilted his head, studying the side of her neck. "You really got those everywhere, didn't you?"

He pulled out a leaf that was trapped in the collar of her sweater.

She held her breath while his hand lingered on her skin. Then exhaled in disappointment when it was gone.

"Any more?" he asked, eyes blazing.

"Gavin," she said, a one-word warning.

His eyes were brooding now. "Why didn't you warn me how addictive you are, Allison Bennett?"

She didn't answer. What could she say, when the situation before them was as hopeless as ever?

GAVIN HAD EXPECTED that it would take a while to establish his reputation as an architect around Squam Lake, but he'd failed to consider the economic surge in home construction—particularly for recreational properties. The following morning, after several meetings with prospective clients, he found himself with two extra projects on his agenda.

Gavin took his foot off the accelerator as he left the highway. His route home led him down Main Street, and he slowed his speed even further as he passed Allison's shop.

Missing her had become a constant pain. But the day before, at least, they'd agreed to be friends and neighbors. Was it possible they could extend that relationship to include business, as well?

It wasn't just his own desire to spend time with her that was motivating him. He knew she'd do a great job on the interior design of the projects he'd just taken on.

Maybe she'd turn him down. But it couldn't hurt to ask.

He pulled into a parking space, locked the wagon and crossed the street to her shop. A group of tourists was just leaving, and he stood to the side to allow the various shoppers to pass. Their Perfect Thing shopping bags were stuffed to the brims.

Inside, Allison was helping another customer at the till. She looked up at the sound of the door chimes. The welcoming smile forming on her face vanished at the sight of Gavin. He followed her gaze as it shifted to the back of the shop.

Though he could only see her from behind, he recognized Marianne right away. She was taking down one of her paintings, obviously not happy with the location Allison had chosen for it.

Crap. He hesitated and considered backing out before Marianne noticed him. But Allison's customer was leaving and now Allison was looking at him with a "Well, what do *you* want" expression. Hoping Marianne would continue to be too absorbed to look this way, he approached the sales counter.

"Looks like you've had a profitable morning."

Allison acknowledged the truth of this with a curt nod.

He wanted to tell her how lovely she looked, but he figured that wouldn't go over too well right now.

"Must be a good day for both of us." He was practically whispering, so that Marianne wouldn't realize he was here. His low tone had the added benefit of causing Allison to shift a few inches closer to him.

"I signed two new clients this morning," he added.

"Congratulations," she said, her tone flat. He guessed that Marianne's presence was behind her unfriendly mood. She hadn't been like this when they'd been raking leaves.

"I was wondering if you'd like to team up with me on the jobs. I think you'll be intrigued, when you hear what they want. One client is a mystery novelist who's looking to build a private writing retreat."

Her eyes rounded. "Really?"

He checked a smile. "The other is a chef from Hartford. He needs a fully equipped kitchen for testing recipes."

"Oh, Gavin."

"I'm sure you'll have some innovative ideas for that one." He could see that he'd succeeded in tempting her.

"Working together. It doesn't seem like the smartest idea."

"Why not? We make a good team. You know it."

She shot him a hostile look. "Yes, I do. And that's the problem."

She had another problem, too, of course. And that was the projects. They were just too exciting for her to turn down. He watched as she fought a battle with herself.

"I suppose we wouldn't need to spend much time together. We could use the phone and e-mail when communication is necessary."

He didn't want her to be finding ways for them to avoid one another. What he wanted...

"Ohhh!"

He whipped his head around at the sound of Marianne's cry. Just in time to see one of her paintings crash to the floor.

CHAPTER SEVENTEEN

GAVIN RUSHED to help Marianne. He checked the canvas for damage, and seeing none, rehung it on the wall.

"Gavin?" Marianne sounded surprised to see him. "What are you doing here?"

Allison folded her arms over her chest as she watched the interplay. Nice act. She was certain that Marianne had noticed Gavin in the store and then intentionally created a ruckus in order to interrupt their conversation.

"The better question is what are you doing here?" Gavin countered. "I thought we agreed you were going to keep your feet up today?"

They sounded like a bickering married couple. Well, wasn't that what they were? Practically. After all, as Gavin had so pointedly noted, they had a child together.

The door chime sounded again, giving Allison

a ready excuse to escape the situation. She approached her new customer, who informed her that he was "only looking." After that, she fussed with a display and then returned to the sales counter.

Gavin approached her. "We'll talk about the new projects later, okay?"

"Sure." The excitement she'd been feeling earlier had vanished. Maybe she was being needlessly insecure, but she felt certain Marianne would find some way to keep the two of them from working together.

She opened an order book, anxious to distract herself as Gavin offered Marianne a lift back to his house.

"I need a few more minutes here." Marianne was still fussing with the painting, adjusting it one inch in one direction, only to slide it back in the opposite direction a moment later.

"Okay. How about I pick up the mail and meet you back at the car." He turned to Allison again. "Let me know when you've made up your mind about the business thing."

Allison gave him a stiff smile. Did he have any idea how much this hurt, witnessing their little domestic interchange?

The other customer in the shop followed Gavin out, leaving Allison and Marianne alone. Allison pulled out a stack of invoices that required her attention. A few minutes later, she sensed someone standing in front of her.

"I'm finished here," Marianne said. "Now that they aren't hidden in the back, they should sell quickly."

Allison glanced at the paintings. Marianne had moved them all to the most prominent positions in the store. She wasn't happy about that, but she wasn't about to argue.

"If they sell, you'll be the first to know." And if they didn't in a few weeks, she was going to move them out of the limelight again.

Marianne acknowledged her comment with a nod. Then she leaned forward confidently. "I wasn't sure how I was going to feel about spending so much time back in Squam Lake. But it's got its good points. And now that Gavin's living here, well, I don't have to sell you on him, do I?"

Allison stared rigidly at the order form in front of her. "No, you don't."

"I saw the look on your face when he asked you to work with him. You're going to, right?"

Grudgingly she admitted, "I'm thinking about it."

"Well, think hard. Feeling about him the way you do, a clean break might be easier."

"Gee, thanks for the advice, Marianne."

"You're being sarcastic. You think I'm the bad guy here, but remember—I knew him first."

"Yes. And you left him."

Marianne looked at her blankly. She just didn't get it.

"I know you don't love him, Marianne. Why are you doing this? Why come back now? And to him? Is it just because I wanted him, that you decided you had to get him back?"

It was the same old pattern. Only suddenly Allison realized what was behind it. The man that Marianne *really* wanted was the one she'd never had.

"You think I went to all this trouble only to hurt you? I couldn't help getting sick, Allison."

"Maybe not. But you didn't need to go running to Gavin. You know my father," she swallowed before adding, "*our* father…would have let you stay with him."

Marianne looked shocked.

"You didn't think I knew?" Allison wasn't about to let on that she'd only recently figured it out.

"Even I was never sure. My mother once told me that Mr. Bennett was my father. But she was drunk, so who knows. Then your grandmother left me that money. Mom told me she felt sorry for me. But I wondered. And I hoped."

"Have you ever asked him?"

"Oh, I couldn't do that." She sounded shocked at the idea. And Allison realized that the one person Marianne would never risk alienating was the one person who had abandoned her.

For the first time in her life, Allison was genuinely able to do what her father had asked her. She felt sorry for Marianne.

GAVIN'S FAMILY ARRIVED on the morning of Tory's birthday. Allison had been dusting in her living room when a dark Audi pulled into the Gray driveway, and she stopped working to stare unabashedly.

First out from the backseat was a big, muscular man. He had several inches on Gavin, and the sort of chest and shoulders that turned heads in a gym.

That had to be Nick, the cop.

Next out was the driver. He had Gavin's lanky

build, but with a more conservative haircut and dark-framed glasses. This had to be the eldest brother, Matthew, the big-shot criminal lawyer. He went around the car and opened the front passenger door. Both men hovered as a petite woman with fluffy gray hair stepped out.

They each took an arm and started for the front door, but they hadn't made it far before Gavin and Tory rushed out to meet them. Allison stepped away from the window as the family members hugged one another.

About an hour later, her phone rang. It was Gavin.

"The party doesn't start until five, but I was wondering if you could come over earlier. My family is anxious to meet you and Tory keeps asking when you're coming."

Allison wasn't looking forward to being at the party with Marianne. At the same time, she wouldn't dream of disappointing Tory. Especially on her birthday. "I'll be over as soon as I can," she promised.

The family was gathered on the deck when she arrived about half an hour later. Allison was relieved to note that Marianne wasn't with them. In the yard below, a piñata was hanging on a low branch of one of Gavin's big trees. Four little girls were dancing around it, one of them Tory. When she spotted Allison, she came running.

"Happy birthday, Tory." Allison gave her a warm hug.

"I'm seven now," Tory told her proudly. "Uncle Nick brought me a piñata, and my friends are going to help break it. It's full of candy," she added in a whisper.

"How exciting," Allison whispered back. "Will you save me a piece?"

Tory nodded solemnly, before running back to join her friends.

Gavin came over and put a hand against the small of her back. "Mom, I'd like you to meet my friend and next-door neighbor, Allison Bennett."

His mother responded politely, shaking Allison's hand and asking a few generic questions.

"Yes, I have lived here all my life." Allison settled into the chair next to his mother and leaned closer to hear her. "Have you seen the movie *On Golden Pond?* It was filmed on Squam Lake."

"Really? That's one of my favorites. I've always loved Katharine Hepburn."

Gavin's mother actually looked a little like the iconic actress, though she was smaller in stature.

When Allison told her this, the older woman absolutely beamed.

The bigger brother, the one who looked like a cop, said, "Good thing she didn't compare you to Henry Fonda, Mom."

"That's my brother Nick," Gavin said, as a belated introduction. "And the other goon is Matthew."

Matthew rose from his chair and came to shake her hand. "Nice to meet you. May I offer you a drink?"

Allison stood, too. "I'd like some iced tea, but I can help myself," she insisted. Matthew followed her into the kitchen anyway.

"So how do you like Squam Lake?" she asked Matthew, making conversation as he filled a glass for her.

"It's a beautiful place. And Tory is looking great. I was worried when Gavin told me he was moving here. The last thing my brother needs is Marianne back in his life. Not now, when he and Tory have finally begun to heal."

Allison couldn't have agreed more. "But that is why he came here. He seems to think that Tory needs her mother."

"Tory has always needed her mother. Unfortunately, Marianne is emotionally incapable of fulfilling that role. As far as I could tell, she was as much a child as Tory and Samantha were. For a change, I'd like to see my brother with a woman who didn't need him to look after her."

Matthew's gaze flashed over her again, and Allison could feel him assessing and judging.

"So, where is Marianne?" she asked, hoping the question sounded casual.

"She was supposed to be here, but half an hour ago she claimed she had an appointment and left. Gavin wasn't too pleased, but she should be back shortly."

"Unfortunately." This was said by Nick, who'd just joined them in the kitchen. He grinned and Allison had a feeling that his smile went far with most of the women he met.

"Claws in, Nick," Matthew said in a warning tone.

"Why? You think Allison is a fan of Marianne's? You grew up with the girl, right?"

Allison nodded. "Yes. We were once friends."

"That must have been fun."

"Nick. I'm warning you."

"It's okay," Allison assured them. "Marianne and I haven't been close for years."

"How about you and Gavin?"

"Nick. Back off, already." Matthew snapped a tea towel at him. Nick howled, then grabbed a towel of his own and soon a war had broken out between the two brothers. In the midst of it, Gavin walked in.

"What the heck? I thought I told you guys I wanted to impress this woman?" He shooed his brothers outside. "The kids are ready to break into that piñata and, Nick, you promised to supervise."

Once they'd left, he turned to Allison. "I came to rescue you."

"I didn't need rescuing. Your brothers are pretty candid, but they're also perfectly charming."

"I think it's the perfectly charming part that has me worried. Come on, let's go. Tory wouldn't want us to miss this."

The other adults stood at the railing watching as Nick gave each of the girls a turn at swinging a plastic bat at the colorful papier-mâché donkey. As they waited for their turns, the girls jumped with excitement.

"Tory looks happy, doesn't she?" Gavin murmured into Allison's ear.

"Yes." It was turning out to be a perfect birthday party. Only where was Marianne? She noticed Gavin checking his watch, as if he was wondering the same thing.

Whack!

The four girls squealed as the piñata crashed to the ground, candy scattering everywhere.

"Good job, Brittany!"

One of Tory's friends had managed to bring the papier-mâché donkey down, and now the girls fell to their knees to gather up the loot.

Once the excitement was over, Gavin started the barbecue, and soon they were eating burgers and salad. When it was time for the cake, Allison noticed Gavin glancing at his watch again.

Marianne's absence at her own daughter's party was absolutely unforgivable as far as Allison was concerned. She could tell Gavin was annoyed, as well. The candles had been blown out and everyone was eating dessert when Marianne finally appeared.

"Everyone having fun?"

Gavin got up, his mouth set in a grim line, to pull out a chair for her. But to Allison's amazement, Marianne just ignored him and headed up the stairs, presumably to her room.

The adults were dumbfounded, but fortunately none of the children noticed anything amiss. Tory passed her father her plate. "Can I have another piece, please?"

That snapped Gavin back to the present. "Sure, squirt. Anyone else?"

As conversation resumed, Allison wondered if the other adults had noticed the fact that Marianne had been drinking.

WHEN SHE GOT HOME after Tory's party, Allison phoned her father. It didn't take long for her to realize he was upset.

"Did Marianne visit you today?"

"How did you know?"

She thought of Marianne's glazed eyes, the wobble in her step. "Just a guess."

Her father gave a characteristic sigh. Which meant he wasn't planning to tell her anything. Allison decided she might as well try the approach that had worked with her mother. The direct approach.

"I phoned Mom this week, Dad. She confirmed what I asked you about the other night."

"What?" He sounded appalled. "Your mother and I had an agreement. We weren't going to get you involved in our mess."

In *his* mess, Allison amended silently. "Did

Marianne ask you to acknowledge her as your daughter, Dad?" That was the only reason she could think of as an explanation for Marianne's inebriated state. In all the time she'd known Marianne, she'd never seen her drink to excess before.

"That has never been proven," her father said. "I won't have you talk that way to me."

"Do you think you're being fair to Marianne?"

"I've tried to watch out for that girl. I've done more than most men would."

Allison's heart sank. This was a side of her father she would have done anything not to have seen.

He had to know that a DNA test could easily give Marianne her proof. And maybe he would be vindicated by such a test. But whether he truly was Marianne's biological father or not was hardly the point.

The fact was, apparently he could have been. And that had been enough to drive away his wife.

But it wouldn't drive away Allison. Despite all of this, he was still her father.

"We don't have to talk about it anymore, Dad." She'd been wrong to raise the subject with him, she saw now. Her mother had tried to warn her. "See you on Tuesday for dinner?"

There was a short silence, then the sound of him clearing his throat. "Sounds good, Allie. You bring the main course and I'll buy a cake for dessert."

THE DAY AFTER THE PARTY, Gavin's family drove back to Hartford. He spent the afternoon doing laundry and cleaning up the kitchen. Marianne slept until late afternoon. When she showed up in the kitchen around three to grab a glass of juice, Tory was upstairs playing in her room.

All day long Gavin had been steaming mad at Marianne, but now he willed himself to be calm. "So what happened last night?"

"What do you mean?" Marianne sat down with her glass, and then reached for one of the muffins in a bowl on the table.

"You missed Tory's birthday party. And when you did show up, you were drunk."

She shook her head, not looking at him. "I had something important to take care of."

"Really? And it couldn't have waited for any time other than Tory's party?"

"Look, Gavin, I know you wanted me to go to that thing, but Tory didn't care, and your family, frankly, can hardly stand to be in the same room as me. I did everyone a favor by staying away last night."

He wanted to argue, but the fact was she spoke the truth. "You can't just show up after six years and expect everything to be all warm and fuzzy. If you want to have a relationship with your daughter, you're going to have to work at it."

Marianne said nothing to that, just stared out the window. Gavin waited several minutes, then lost his patience and went downstairs to take a load of clean clothes out of the dryer.

He didn't see Marianne again until dinnertime. He'd prepared a roast chicken, and for someone so thin, she managed to put away a good amount. As he encouraged her to drink a glass of milk, he realized he was treating her like a child.

And that was the way she seemed to him. She'd become someone he needed to look after. And she didn't mean much more than that to him.

Certainly, he was no longer affected by her beauty. It had become an abstract notion to him, much like looking at a model on the cover of a magazine. There was simply no sense of connection.

And he didn't think Tory felt any connection, either. She tolerated their guest's presence, but that was all. Marianne's performance at the party had pretty much eliminated, in his mind, the possibility that there would ever be a mother-daughter connection.

But then again, maybe Marianne was right and a party wasn't the place to begin. What Tory and Marianne needed was more time between just the two of them.

When dinner was over, he said, "I'll do the dishes tonight. Why don't you and Tory read books for a while."

Tory obligingly went to pick out some stories, but Marianne stayed where she was.

"I'm not really into kiddie stories, Gavin."

He held back a sarcastic rejoinder and tried to see the situation from her point of view. "Tory has some well-written books. Try one. You might be pleasantly surprised."

Marianne gave a resigned shrug, then pulled herself out of her chair and headed slowly for the living room. By the time she'd settled into the sofa, Tory was back with a pile of books. Gavin picked out one filled with award-winning illustrations.

"Try this," he suggested, before heading back to the kitchen. As he loaded the dishwasher and wiped down the counters, he listened to Marianne reading the story that he'd read so often he had the words memorized.

As did Tory. Whenever Marianne hesitated, she ended up filling in the gaps.

By the end, Tory was doing most of the reading. When it finished, Marianne said, "Okay. I guess you'd better pick another book."

"No, thanks."

He was surprised by Tory's answer. Usually she was insatiable when it came to story time. He was about to intervene, when he glanced out the kitchen window and noticed Allison walking toward his house.

He smoothed his hair, then went to the front door. Allison was wearing a moss-green sweater, the color of her eyes, and jeans. Nothing fancy, but she looked absolutely gorgeous to him.

"Hey, there." He held the door with one hand, unsure about inviting her in. If Marianne hadn't been home, he would have done so in a heartbeat. He was so pleased to see her.

Her smile was brilliant and uncomplicated, just like in the old days, before Marianne had come on the scene.

"I've been thinking about those projects," she said.

Was she going to turn him down? Surely not with a smile like that. "And...?"

"I'd love to work on them with you."

"I'm glad." He couldn't stop himself from reaching out to push a strand of hair back from her face.

"Why are you touching me?"

His heart skipped a beat, but there was no accusation in her words, he realized. It was just a question.

"Because I want to," he answered honestly. He wanted to touch much more than just her hair. He studied her sweet lips, the smooth skin of her neck, the swelling of her breasts behind the cover of her sweater.

He took her hand. "I know I'm not supposed to talk to you this way. But I've missed you."

"What about Marianne?" Allison's gaze shifted beyond him.

He turned, then started. Marianne was right behind him, eyes narrowed. She put her hands on her hips as she looked from him to Allison, then back again.

Marianne's hand settled on Gavin's shoulder. Her fingers gripped him tightly.

"Are you finished out here? I need to talk to

you for a second." She lowered her voice. "It's about our daughter."

"I should go." Allison tugged her hand free and backed down the stairs.

"Please wait." He'd seen the flash of calculation in Marianne's eyes, and he'd heard it in her voice, too. This was the first time she'd referred to Tory as *their* daughter. Clearly this maternal act was for Allison's sake. The idea that Marianne would use Tory like that, as a pawn in a game of one-upmanship with Allison, made him absolutely livid.

He shifted Marianne's hand from his shoulder. "It can wait. I need to talk to Allison right now."

Anger flared red on Marianne's cheeks. "This is important, Gavin."

"When it comes to *my* daughter, I know what's important. Now why don't you…" He was about to say something really rude, when a little voice stopped him.

"Daddy?"

Clutching one of her picture books to her chest, Tory slipped by Marianne to reach him. She scowled at Marianne. "I don't want her to read to me anymore. She said I had to let her, but I don't want to."

"Don't look at me that way," Marianne said. "I didn't do anything wrong. I can't help it if…"

"Marianne. I'd really prefer it if we could talk about this later." Five more minutes with Allison. Was that too much to ask?

But apparently it was, because Tory had just spied Allison, too. She broke out a huge smile. "I want Allison to read me my stories, Daddy."

The woman and the little girl moved toward one another, as naturally as if they belonged together. Allison took the proffered book. "This looks like a fun story. Where should we go to read it?"

"My bedroom," Tory said. "Excuse me, Daddy."

Gavin watched as they went inside, passing Marianne on their way to the stairs.

Marianne raked a hand through her hair, clearly frustrated. "She's very temperamental, isn't she? I don't know why…" She kept talking, but Gavin tuned her out.

Something important had just happened here, he realized. His daughter had made her first decision since Sam's death.

And he couldn't approve more of her taste.

CHAPTER EIGHTEEN

WHEN SHE REALIZED Gavin wasn't paying any attention to her, Marianne went up to her room. Gavin made coffee, then took a mug out to the deck. After about twenty minutes Marianne joined him there. She had an icy calm about her.

"This isn't working out, is it?"

Tory and Allison were still upstairs, reading. He wondered how much longer they would be. He was getting desperate to finish his conversation with Allison. He bit back on his impatience and tried to focus on what Marianne had just said.

"We've hit a few rough patches in the past few days," he admitted. "You're used to living on your own and Tory and I aren't used to having an extra roommate, either. It's going to require a little give-and-take on both sides."

"A roommate." Marianne's smile was one-sided. "Is that how you see me?"

Her question surprised him. "What did you expect?"

"Maybe that we would be a family."

"Seriously? Do you really think you want that?"

She turned away from him and went to lean over the railing. The lake was tranquil, glowing with the reflection of the setting sun. "Did she suffer, Gavin?"

It was the first time she'd spoken of Sam. Gavin's throat tightened. He took a sip of coffee, waiting until he could be sure of his voice. "No."

Marianne must have been holding her breath, because he heard her expel a long sigh. "Good." Her tone became brisk. "I'd like to make a phone call, if that's all right."

"Of course."

She started for the patio door, then paused. "She always had the one man I wanted most in the world, you know."

She couldn't mean Sam.

"Are you talking about Allison?"

"I just realized it the other day, when I was at her store. I think we figured it out at the same time."

Who the hell was this man she was talking about? Not him, surely. He'd only met Allison this summer.

"I think it's going to be easier, now that I understand."

"Marianne, I wish like hell that *I* understood a word you were saying."

"Ask Allison. She'll explain it to you."

AN HOUR LATER, Allison and Tory were still up in Tory's bedroom. Gavin couldn't stand it any longer. He went to check on them and found them both asleep, Tory under the covers and Allison on top, an open picture book resting in her lap.

He took one of the extra blankets and settled it gently over Allison, then tiptoed out of the room. Marianne was in the hallway, lugging her suitcase toward the stairs. Through the open doorway to her room, he saw her two cardboard boxes packed and waiting.

He took the suitcase from her. "Where are you going?"

She didn't meet his eyes. "I've asked a friend to pick me up."

"You don't have to leave."

"Thanks. But I think it's best."

Gavin carried the suitcase down to the front door, then went back for the boxes. By the time he'd brought them both down, a dark sedan was pulling up to the house. A graying man, tall and broad shouldered, got out.

"Marianne?" he asked, his tone hopeful.

Gavin turned a questioning eye to the woman beside him.

"He owns an art gallery in North Conway," she said by means of an explanation. "His name is Shane O'Brien. He's a good guy."

Was this about business? Maybe. But the gleam in Shane's eyes told Gavin it probably was more than just that. "How old is this guy?"

"Not that old. In his late forties, I think."

Almost twenty years older than she was. "Are you sure about this?"

She nodded. "He'll take care of me."

Shane was already bounding toward them. He shook Gavin's hand as Marianne introduced them. Gavin could tell he was curious, but he asked no questions, just grabbed Marianne's suitcase quickly, as if afraid she might change her mind.

Gavin took the boxes, piling them into the trunk next to the suitcase. Shane closed the trunk firmly, then dusted off his hands. "Ready?"

When Marianne nodded, he opened the passenger door for her. Marianne hesitated before getting inside. "Thanks, Gavin."

He gave her a hug and refrained from commenting again on how thin she was. "Take care of yourself."

"I will."

"Promise?"

"I'll make sure she does," Shane said. He looked relieved when she finally slid into his car.

Gavin watched them drive away with a mixture of regret and relief. Then he went back inside and climbed the stairs to his daughter's room.

THE SOUND OF CAR DOORS slamming woke Allison from her sleep. She was in Tory's bed. She set aside the book she was still holding on to, and removed the blanket that Gavin must have covered her with.

From outside, she heard a car drive away, then the sound of the front door closing. She sat up, careful not to disturb Tory. A moment later, Gavin appeared in the doorway.

"You fell asleep." His eyes were light and full of tenderness and warmth.

"Sorry." She folded the blanket. "Where's Marianne?"

"Gone."

"What?"

"A friend of hers just picked her up. I'll give you the whole story later. Want a cup of coffee? I just…"

"Allison?" Tory asked sleepily.

She'd been doing her best to creep out of Tory's room, but the little girl had woken anyway. She sat up in her bed, rubbed her eyes. "Daddy?"

Gavin came into the room. "I'll handle this," he told Allison. Going over to his daughter's bed, he tucked her under the covers again. "Go back to sleep, squirt. It's bedtime."

Tory blinked sleepily. "Allison read me lots of stories."

"I'm glad."

She turned to the picture on her nightstand and so did Gavin. A younger, healthier Marianne, with shorter hair but the same aloof expression, stared back at them, her arms full with her infant twins.

"That's her, isn't it?" Tory asked.

Gavin shot Allison a worried look before answering honestly. "Yes."

"She's my mom."

"Yes, she is."

"Is that why she's living with us?"

"Actually, she's left now, Tory. She's gone to live with another friend."

Now what? Was his daughter going to freak out? For years she'd lived without a mother. And now that she'd found her, Marianne had left just as suddenly as she'd arrived.

But Tory's reaction was calm. "That's okay. Allison isn't going anywhere, right?"

"No, I'm not. Go to sleep, Tory. I'll see you in the morning."

With a smile on her face, Tory finally sank back into her pillow. She was asleep even as Gavin kissed her forehead. Allison held the door for him, and he took her hand as soon as he was close enough.

"Come out to the deck with me?"

She followed him willingly.

"Finally alone." He groaned, then took her into his arms and kissed her.

Desire flamed, as he wrapped his arms around her waist and pulled her body close to his. She pulled her mouth from his to ask, "You didn't kick her out, did you?"

Much as she was glad the other woman was gone, she didn't think she could live with that.

"No. She decided to go on her own. But not before she said something rather cryptic about you and she being in love with the same man for a long time. Do you know what she meant by that?"

Allison nodded.

"Want to clue me in?"

"Marianne and I are half sisters. The man she was referring to is our father." She almost laughed at Gavin's shocked expression.

"You're kidding."

"I wish. I just found out this week. My mom finally admitted that the reason she divorced my dad was because she'd found out he'd had an affair with Marianne's mother."

"Wow. That's unbelievable."

"Want to hear the details?"

"Another time." He stroked her forehead, his gaze heated and focused intently on her.

Allison could tell he had one thing on his mind. But she needed to make sure of a few things first. "Did Marianne give a reason for leaving so suddenly?"

"I think she had the bizarre idea that she was going to move in here and we would become an instant family."

"But it didn't work out that way."

"No. She saw pretty quickly that I was already deeply in love, and it wasn't with her."

Allison's heart skipped. This kind of happiness had been unimaginable just a few hours earlier. "I didn't think I'd ever hear you say those words."

"You're going to hear them so much, you'll probably get sick of them. I love you, Allison Bennett." He framed her face with his hands. "Is it too soon to ask you to marry me?"

This was joy, Allison knew. Life would never offer her more than in this instant. "I love you, too," she promised. "And you know I love Tory."

She would have a husband and a daughter. She couldn't be happier.

"You won't change your mind about *this* wedding?" Gavin teased.

She pulled his mouth down to meet hers. The question didn't deserve an answer. Sometimes you just *know*.

And this was one of those times.

Bundles of Joy—
coming next month to Superromance

Experience the romance, excitement and joy with 6 heartwarming titles.

BABY, I'M YOURS #1476 by *Carrie Weaver*

ANOTHER MAN'S BABY
(The Tulanes of Tennessee)
#1477 by *Kay Stockham*

THE MARINE'S BABY (9 Months Later)
#1478 by *Rogenna Brewer*

BE MY BABIES (Twins)
#1479 by *Kathryn Shay*

THE DIAPER DIARIES (Suddenly a Parent)
#1480 by *Abby Gaines*

HAVING JUSTIN'S BABY (A Little Secret)
#1481 by *Pamela Bauer*

Exciting, Emotional and Unexpected!

*Look for these Superromance titles in March 2008.
Available wherever books are sold.*

HSR71476

HARLEQUIN

More Than Words

"The more I see, the more I feel the need."

—**Aviva Presser,** real-life heroine

*Aviva Presser is a Harlequin More Than Words
award winner and the founder of **Bears Without Borders.***

Discover your inner heroine!

HARLEQUIN

SUPPORTING CAUSES OF CONCERN TO WOMEN
WWW.HARLEQUINMORETHANWORDS.COM

MTW07AP1

REQUEST YOUR FREE BOOKS!

2 FREE NOVELS PLUS 2 FREE GIFTS!

HARLEQUIN®

Super Romance®

Exciting, emotional, unexpected!

YES! Please send me 2 FREE Harlequin Superromance® novels and my 2 FREE gifts. After receiving them, if I don't wish to receive any more books, I can return the shipping statement marked "cancel." If I don't cancel, I will receive 6 brand-new novels every month and be billed just $4.69 per book in the U.S., or $5.24 per book in Canada, plus 25¢ shipping and handling per book and applicable taxes, if any*. That's a savings of close to 15% off the cover price! I understand that accepting the 2 free books and gifts places me under no obligation to buy anything. I can always return a shipment and cancel at any time. Even if I never buy another book from Harlequin, the two free books and gifts are mine to keep forever.   135 HDN EEX7 336 HDN EEYK

Name   (PLEASE PRINT)

Address   Apt.

City   State/Prov.   Zip/Postal Code

Signature (if under 18, a parent or guardian must sign)

Mail to the **Harlequin Reader Service®**:

IN U.S.A.: P.O. Box 1867, Buffalo, NY 14240-1867
IN CANADA: P.O. Box 609, Fort Erie, Ontario L2A 5X3

Not valid to current Harlequin Superromance subscribers.

Want to try two free books from another line?
Call 1-800-873-8635 or visit www.morefreebooks.com.

* Terms and prices subject to change without notice. NY residents add applicable sales tax. Canadian residents will be charged applicable provincial taxes and GST. This offer is limited to one order per household. All orders subject to approval. Credit or debit balances in a customer's account(s) may be offset by any other outstanding balance owed by or to the customer. Please allow 4 to 6 weeks for delivery.

Your Privacy: Harlequin is committed to protecting your privacy. Our Privacy Policy is available online at www.eHarlequin.com or upon request from the Reader Service. From time to time we make our lists of customers available to reputable firms who may have a product or service of interest to you. If you would prefer we not share your name and address, please check here. ☐

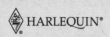

COMING NEXT MONTH

#1476 BABY, I'M YOURS · Carrie Weaver
As a recently widowed mom with three kids, Becca Smith struggles to keep life together. The discovery that she's pregnant is making things worse. There's only o person she can turn to—Rick Jensen. He's her business partner...and possibly this baby's father.

#1477 ANOTHER MAN'S BABY · Kay Stockham
The Tulanes of Tennessee
Landing in the ditch while in premature labor is not on Darcy Rhodes's to-do list. Fortunately, rescue arrives in the form of Garret Tulane. He seems so perfect, he's like Prince Charming. But will they forge their own happily ever after once the snow stops?

#1478 THE MARINE'S BABY · Rogenna Brewer
9 Months Later
Joining the military taught Lucky Calhoun the importance of family. And now he wants one of his own. That wish may come true sooner than planned. Thanks to a mix-up at the sperm bank, Caitlin Calhoun—his half brother's widow—seems to b carrying his child.

#1479 BE MY BABIES · Kathryn Shay
Twins
Simon McCarthy should not be attracted to Lily Wakefield. Not only is she new to town, but also she's pregnant—with twins. Still, the feelings between them make h think about their future together. Then her past catches up and threatens to destroy everything.

#1480 THE DIAPER DIARIES · Abby Gaines
Suddenly a Parent
A baby is so not playboy Tyler Warrington's thing. Still, he must care for the one who appeared on his doorstep. Fine. Hire a nanny. Then Bethany Hart talks her wa into the job—for a cost. Funny, the more time he spends with her, the more willin; he is to pay.

#1481 HAVING JUSTIN'S BABY · Pamela Bauer
Justin Collier has been Paige Stephens's best friend forever. Then one night she tu to him for comfort and...well, everything changes. Worse, she's now pregnant and he's proposing! She's always wanted to marry for love, but can Justin offer her tha

HSRCNM0208